About the Author

Frank Dirscherl is the author of many novels, including the Amazon bestselling *The Wraith* and *Sanderson of Metro,* as well as several short stories. His *The Wraith Dread Avenger of the Underworld* books have been enjoyed by readers all over the world.

A librarian with over thirty years experience, Frank has also worked at a book wholesaler, a specialist medical practice and as a tutor in the writing and producing of comic books. His interests include reading, traveling, politics, architecture and the environment.

Frank lives in the Illawarra on the south coast of New South Wales, Australia, with his wife and daughter, and is always working on his latest literary endeavors.

About the Author

Greg Gick is a native of Indiana whose work has appeared in the *Doctor Who* charity anthology *Missing Pieces*, Airship 27's *Mystery Men (And Women)*, *Mars McCoy* and *Secret Agent X* anthologies, as well as Moonstone Comics' *Green Hornet* prose anthologies. He has another Wraith tale coming up in Airship 27's own Wraith anthology, with many other stories in the works.

GLOWING EYES MEDIA

Praise for *Sanderson of Metro*
Amazon bestseller

"Once shrouded in mystery, The Wraith's stunning origin is finally revealed. Dirscherl and Nash have written one hell of an adventure novel filled with myth, intrigue, and excitement. Highly recommended reading."
- A.P. Fuchs, writer, *The Axiom-man Saga, The Way of the Fog, Undead World trilogy*

"Recommended for Wraith and pulp hero fans."
- Leon Mallett, *Amazon*

"At the end of the day, this novel is a worthy addition to The Wraith's continuing story and a necessary purchase if you're a fan of the character. It's also just a flat out enjoyable reading experience."
- Marcus Bucklin, *Amazon*

"The story is well written, and the Paul Sanderson character fleshed out fairly well...I highly recommend this well written entry for all comic book fans."
- Virginia E. Johnson, *Amazon*

Praise for *The Wraith*
Amazon bestseller

"I love the coloring job and specially the 'glowing' eyes on the chest of the character."
- Guillermo del Toro, director, *Blade II, Hellboy I & II*

"I liked the story a lot... It's a very strong debut."
Steve Englehart, writer, *Detective Comics, The Avengers, Green Lantern*

"I have read the novel (I couldn't put it down)... It is amazing to see how her (Leena) character evolves from Part I to Part II. At first she appears as every other 'girlfriend' in an action film, but those twelve months that pass obviously change her as a person and I love the person she becomes: tougher, but still human."
- Amber Moelter, actress, *Catwoman: Copycat*

"I finished *The Wraith* book last night. I must say I enjoyed it quite a bit. The scenes kept playing in my head like a big budget Hollywood film. I mentioned earlier that I enjoy when the hero is put to the test physically and doesn't win the battle unscathed. Boy, (Frank) delivered that in spades!"
- Jeff Welborn, artist, *Nightmare World, The Wraith*

"Genius + sweat + dedication = hard hittin' hero action! Go Aussie!"
- Dan Lennard, writer, *People* magazine

"*The Wraith* is a wonderful throwback to the purple prose of the bloody pulps with a hero clearly descendant from the likes of the Shadow and the Spider. A fast, action-packed thrill-ride with great characters, both noble and villainous. Slam-bang kick off to a super new series. One I'm anxious to follow."

   – Ron Fortier, writer, *The Spider, Brother Bones, Domino Lady*

"I became familiar with Frank Dirscherl's The Wraith from the comic book of the same name. When the first Wraith novel came out I just had to read it. I was not disappointed. The Wraith is a fast-paced thrill-ride. I'm looking forward to the upcoming sequel."

   – Bobby Nash, writer, *Evil Ways, Fantastix, Lance Star*

"*The Wraith* (is) a really fun read. Have been a fan of Kenneth Robeson's Doc Savage and The Avenger books for years... *The Wraith* reminds me of Robeson at his best."

   – G.R. Lawson, Publisher, General Jinjur Comics

"A short, pulp, superhero novel... Clearly more adventures to come with how this is set up."

   – Richard Scott, *Super Reader* website

"*The Wraith* is an enlightening journey into the darkness of superhero fiction, and a worthy entry into both pulpdom and comicdom."

   – Kevin Noel Olson, *Silver Bullet Comics* website

"*The Wraith* is a testament to Frank's dedication and talent. Other small press characters have come and gone, but The Wraith endures, because Frank understands what makes a classic character."

-   Richard Evans, writer, *The Canadian Legion*

"When it comes to superhero fiction and classic pulp stories, Frank Dirscherl channels those classic adventures of the past into *The Wraith* with ease and gives you a hero to believe in."

-   Stephen J. Semones, writer/director, *Beyond the Lens, Crossfire, The Wraith: Eyes of Judgment*

"Frank Dirscherl's writing is action-packed and reminds me why superhero fiction is so much fun in the first place!"

-   A.P. Fuchs, writer, *The Axiom-man Saga, The Way of the Fog, Undead World trilogy*

"Totally enjoyed this book. Good story, a real hero vs villain yarn. Can't wait to read the other adventures of The Wraith."

-   J. Newey, *Amazon*

Praise for *Valley of Evil*

"The second Wraith novel is an improvement, I think. Right from the start Dirscherl throws you into the middle of crazy action.... This book is a whole lot of superheroic pulp fun, and the good news is there seems to be more to come...I look forward to some more of the same."

    – Richard Scott, *Super Reader* website

"I think (Dirscherl) really captured a noir element with (his) voice."

    – Joshua Gamon, writer, *Abigail & Rox, Digital Webbing Presents*

"I did quite enjoy the books. Best of all, it wasn't overly sex-filled or gory—I can't stand most modern superhero comics that show such things or have the heroes just swear and swear. So *The Wraith* (and *Valley of Evil*) was just up my alley."

    – Greg Gick, writer, *The Werewolf of Rutherford Grange, Tales of the Shadowmen, Secret Agent X Vol. 2*

"The Dread Avenger is back. After battling the Cobra in his first prose adventure, The Wraith returns to face all new challenges from Metro City's greatest villains, most notably Hong Kong drug kingpin Ma Tzi. As with his first Wraith novel, Frank Dirscherl treats us to a pulp-inspired adventure that keeps readers on the edge of their seat. You have to read this novel in one sitting."

    – Bobby Nash, writer, *Evil Ways, Fantastix, Lance Star*

"In the past five years there has been a tremendous resurgence in pulp fiction centering on the old heroic pulps. Young writers have started taking up the mantle of old masters like Walter Gibson and Lester Dent and begun creating their own avengers in tales of genuine purple prose. Among the best of this new generation of wordsmiths is Australian, Frank Dirscherl and the exploits of his modern pulp paladin, The Wraith. This is grand pulp!"

– Ron Fortier, writer, *The Spider, Brother Bones, Domino Lady*

Praise for *Crossfire*

"Stephen did a fantastic job of bringing Frank Dirscherl's character to life!"
- Adam DiTroia, composer, *The Wraith: Eyes of Judgment*,
MTV, Fox Sports

"Loved the book!! Can't wait for the next installment..."
- Larry Mainland, actor, *The Walking Dead, Lawless,
The Three Stooges*

"The action comes swift, and doesn't stop until the final pages. *Crossfire* tells a great story of betrayal and revenge."
- C.R. Blevins, writer, *A Western Tale*

"This was my first introduction to The Wraith and I was not disappointed. The action comes swift, and doesn't stop until the final pages.... If you love a good action/hero story, you will certainly enjoy reading *Crossfire.*"
- Ally, *Amazon*

"Makes me want more...should be the next series on Netflix..."
- Bill Lancaster, *Amazon*

"Another excellent entry in The Wraith Adventures series. Thoroughly recommended for Wraith fans and fans of pulp super-heroics."
- Leon Mallett, *Amazon*

Praise for *Cult of the Damned*

"Only by the first three pages, Frank Dirscherl wonderfully captures a dark and mysterious atmosphere, one that leaves the reader with a cryptic and eerie sensation; one that makes me cold just thinking about it."

> – Rennie Cowan, writer/director, *The Thriller Idol: A Tribute to the Legacy of Michael Jackson, Kade the Conqueror*

"Frank Dirscherl pulls you into the world of The Wraith from the first sentence and refuses to let you go until the last one."

> – Stephen J. Semones, writer/director, *Beyond the Lens, Crossfire, The Wraith: Eyes of Judgment*

"The Wraith is one of my favorite characters and every time Frank Dirscherl puts pen to paper I know I'm in for a real treat."

> – A.P. Fuchs, writer, *The Axiom-man Saga, The Way of the Fog, Undead World trilogy*

Praise for *Cry of the Werewolf*

"Frank Dirscherl delivers beyond measure.... The solid characters, settings and story really propel you page to page and leave you hanging on for more."
- Stephen J. Semones, writer/director, *Beyond the Lens, Crossfire, The Wraith: Eyes of Judgment*

"Each new installment in *The Wraith Adventures* series is a guaranteed good time filled with high adventure, romance and pulpy fun. Dirscherl is at the top of his form."
- A.P. Fuchs, writer, *The Axiom-man Saga, The Way of the Fog, Undead World trilogy*

"The writing is well done and well edited, and is filled with that distinct Dirscherl style of pulp that I enjoy so much. The book is a perfect example of what Neo Pulp/Superhero and Horror fiction can be and is a worthy addition to any fan's collection."
- Marcus Bucklin, *Amazon*

Praise for *Vendetta*

"...in all a great brew that had me hooked for the whole ride. Now bring on the next book, Frank..."

- Leon Mallett, *Amazon*

"This book starts with a literal bang and doesn't let the foot off of the gas until the very last page. The book is well plotted and moves at a breakneck pace, making it an enjoyable, short read. I loved this book very much as a fan of The Wraith and I believe that anyone who is a fan of the series should consider this required reading."

- Marcus Bucklin, *Amazon*

Praise for *Zombies Attack!* in *Metahumans vs the Undead*

"This compilation of superheroes vs evil offers top entertainment for superhero lovers! Frank Dirscherl and others are at their best with their contributed stories. I will now pursue other stories written by these authors, such as those involving Mr. Dirscherl's The Wraith. This type of reading enjoyment knows no end!"

– Ramona Wingart, writer, *Where is Brother Beaver?*, *Emily Suzanne Smith!*

Praise for *Werewolves Attack!* in *Metahumans vs Werewolves*

"Always a great read. Can never put it down once you get started... "

– Geraldine L. Lewis, *Amazon*

BY FRANK DIRSCHERL

FICTION

The Wraith Dread Avenger of the Underworld series

Sanderson of Metro (with Bobby Nash)
Serpent Rising (with Greg Gick)
The Wraith
Valley of Evil
Crossfire (with Stephen J. Semones)
Cult of the Damned
Cry of the Werewolf
Swamp Witch of Satan's Forest (with Ray MacKay) - COMING SOON
Vendetta
Lady Wraith (with Adam Oravec) - COMING SOON

SHORT STORY COLLECTIONS

Metahumans vs. the Undead
Metahumans vs. Werewolves
Metahumans vs. Robots
Metahumans vs. the Ultimate Evil
Lance Star – Sky Ranger Vol. 1

NON-FICTION

The Wraith: Eyes of Judgment – The Official Script Book & Movie Guide
(with Stephen J. Semones)
The Hitchers of Oz
Beyond the Lens (edited)

www.glowingeyesmedia.com

BY GREG GICK

FICTION

The Wraith Dread Avenger of the Underworld series

Serpent Rising (with Frank Dirscherl)

SHORT STORY COLLECTIONS

Missing Pieces
Mars McCoy
Mystery Men (And Women)
Secret Agent XZ
The Green Hornet
The Wraith Dread Avenger of the Underworld Vol. 1

SERPENT RISING

Books of Judgment Book Two
a Wraith tale

by

Frank Dirscherl & Greg Gick

GLOWING EYES MEDIA
WOLLONGONG

GLOWING EYES MEDIA
PO Box 31
Wollongong NSW 2520

This book is a work of fiction. Names, characters, places and events either are products of the author's imagination or are used fictitiously. Any resemblance to actual events or persons living or dead is purely coincidental.

ISBN 978-0-6457475-9-1

SERPENT RISING
Serpent Rising is Copyright © 2023 by Frank Dirscherl. All Rights Reserved, including the right to reproduce in whole or in part in any form. The Wraith Dread Avenger of the Underworld and Glowing Eyes Media are Copyright © and Trademark ® 2023 by Frank Dirscherl. All Rights Reserved.

PUBLISHED BY GLOWING EYES MEDIA, March 2023
www.glowingeyesmedia.com
FRONT COVER ART by Malcolm McClinton
COVER LAYOUT AND DESIGN AND INTERIOR DESIGN by Frank Dirscherl
EDITED by Frank & Jennifer Dirscherl
FIRST PUBLISHED IN 2017.
SECOND EDITION

For more on *Serpent Rising*
visit www.glowingeyesmedia.com

Text set in Garamond-Normal. Printed and bound in the USA

A catalogue record for this book is available from the National Library of Australia

The Wraith Dread Avenger of the Underworld series
in correct reading order (including short stories)

- *The Wraith*
- *Sanderson of Metro*
- *Serpent Rising*
- *Valley of Evil*
- *Crossfire*
- *Cult of the Damned*
- *The Things I Love the Most* in *Metahumans vs the Ultimate Evil*
- *Cry of the Werewolf*
- *Werewolves Attack!* in *Metahumans vs Werewolves*
- *Sundown* in *The Wraith Dread Avenger of the Underworld*
- *Swamp Witch of Satan's Forest* - COMING SOON
- *Vendetta*
- *Lady Wraith* - COMING SOON
- *Robots Attack!* in *Metahumans vs Robots*
- *Zombies Attack!* in *Metahumans vs the Undead*

So far...but the story goes on...

To all you Wraith fans–this completes the secret origin stories you've long been clamoring for - FD

To Frank, for letting me play in his sandbox. And to my mother, for always believing in me even when I didn't - GG

SERPENT RISING

~ Chapter 1 ~

"HE'S COMING!" the voice cried out.

Lydia Hughes, the nurse at the station, caught her breath, shuddering.

The words, high and strained, reverberated off the walls. The air quivered with their raw tempo. Yet she knew their point of origin was merely a hall away.

"GODS! HE'S COMING!!!"

Lydia glanced toward the desk intercom, wondering if she should summon her superior. Charge Nurse Dalmyre, ostensibly the staff member in charge that night, was somewhere else at present. That was not unusual. Old Lady Dalmyre always preferred to be *somewhere else* than her post. Usually in one of the more disused storerooms with her fat legs curled around Dr. Foster's hips.

"HE'S COMMMMMINNNNGGGGG!!!!"

Lydia was stationed on the fourth floor of the Metro City Hospital for the Criminally Insane. She had thought she'd known what she was getting into when she took the job. She quickly realized she had no idea. Hindsight was a bitch.

A contemptuous snort drew her attention. "Aw, it's just the Chink in 416 again, baby." Perched—*sloshed* was a better word, with fat rolls of his fleshly posterior hanging drooped like anchored curtains over the seat of his chair—the security guard in his rumpled, stained uniform gave her another of his lecherous leers. "He's always yellin' his trap off like that." His eyes ran over Lydia like those of a sex-starved animal. "Don't pay it no mind."

Lydia *did* mind, though. And she minded being in this disgusting guard's obese presence. Jess took great pleasure in comparing her to *that chick from Pirates of the Caribbean, only with actual boobies.* That was one of his more repeatable comments. Lydia did indeed look much like actress Keira Knightley, and was rather shapely. But she didn't need to be reminded of it loudly and repeatedly. Particularly by a three-hundred-pound lout that made Donald Trump look like a pious eunuch.

The first five or six times he had propositioned her, she had filed a sexual harassment complaint with Human Resources. By the time he reached nine, she had stopped. It did no good to complain about wrongs in Metro City. *We're short staffed, we can't afford to lose personnel of his experience* was the consistent reply.

A year ago, when Lydia first arrived in town, from country Vermont, college diploma in hand and big dreams in her head, she was just like a thousand other high-minded young idealists who poured into Metro City every year. They knew that Metro was the worst hovel of crime, poverty and despair on the eastern seaboard, if not the entire United States, but that was why they had come. To make a difference. To change this city for the better. And, like it or not, that's where the jobs were.

Thus, they took one-room apartments with impossibly-high rent, volunteered at legal aid offices and homeless shelters, started up free clinics and soup kitchens. To help lift the poor and forgotten in the city. To stand against the forces of corruption and vice and make Metro City into the glorious example of hope and vision they knew it could be.

Most washed their hands of the place within six months. If they even lasted that long. They had quickly learned the one lesson about Metro that could not, would not, change. And that was Metro City had no absolutely no intention of becoming any better. Why should it? Gangs ran freely in the streets, drugs were sold openly in school bathrooms and hallways. Anything and everything illicit was available for the right price. Worse than New York, worse than Chicago, worse than any other city you could name.

But the rich and powerful were too busy making money hand over fist from that very corruption to worry about it, and the poor were either too busy trying to snatch what the other fellow had to care, or doing just about anything to merely survive. Everybody knew, next to nobody gave a damn. That was just the way things were. Kindness and charity had little place in this city. Only one law prevailed on Metro's arch and feculent streets: grab what you could get, however you could get it, and everyone could go to blazes.

As for the young nurse herself, bit by bit she was saving whatever she could. As soon as she was able, she intended to leave her job, and the city, in her dust. Country Vermont never sounded so good. Part of her hated to go. The Hospital needed all the help it could get. Like most other *funded* institutions in Metro, it was understaffed and under-equipped, barely allocated enough cash by state and city to keep the electricity running. Much of the rest was squandered by a bevvy of directors, managers and the like. The Metro City Hospital for the Criminally Insane wasn't truly an institution designed to help cure the mentally ill...it was a convenient dumping ground for those the City Fathers preferred to be disposed of as quickly and quietly as possible.

"HE'S COMING!"

Lydia shuddered again. *That poor man in 416, he spent all day and night screaming his lungs out.*

"HE'S COMING! HE'S COMING! OH GODS—HE'S COMING!!!"

Jess shifted uncomfortably, his triple-chins reverberating. Even he was becoming annoyed. "Slant-eyed nut. Taser his yellow hide if he don't shut up soon."

Lydia sighed, pushed her chair away from her desk, and bent to retrieve a report that had tumbled to the floor. She simply could not wait to get out of there. It was a shame, but what else could she do? In the end, a girl had to look after herself. Metro City corrupted everyone. Even her in time, she felt sure.

Curling her fingers around the fallen report, Lydia heard footsteps. Someone was coming into the ward. Charge Nurse Dalmyre? No, her stride was a familiar one, a sort of clod-hopping shuffle, totally unique. She heard Jess's feet hit the floor as he wobbled his way out of his chair. He stumbled forward and rounded the corner out of Lydia's sight. He never would have bothered if it was Dalmyre. "Hey," she heard Jess's voice bark, "who the hell are..."

416 continued shouting. "HE'S COMING! HE'S COMING! HE'S CUH—"

And then...silence.

Dead silence.

Both 416 and Jess as quiet as the grave.

Lydia blinked. That was weird. But whomever had entered was approaching, though still out of view. A strong, purposeful gait. She rose straight, put on her best smile, and started automatically, even before the stranger had appeared. "Hello. May I help you?"

A dark shape emerged from his vantage point.

And Lydia Hughes' world went white.

* * * * * *

"HE'S COMING!"

The man in 416 screeched and howled. He gibbered and slobbered. His lips were crimson, drenched with drool. His hair was waist-long, unwashed and greasy. Constrained in his ragged straitjacket, he threw himself against the sodden, yellowed padded fabric of his cell, eyes bulging as he cried out the same words again and again and again. But he was not insane. He knew that. He also knew his master was returning. Soon. Very soon.

"HE'S COMING!"

No one knew his name, he was aware. He overheard the staff refer to him as Patient 416. Many others in the hospital referred to him as simply the Chink. In fact, he knew–remembered–that he was Mongolian. Halh to be precise. Three years ago, he had been found amid the rubble of the Philadelphia World's Fair. He proved unresponsive to interrogation or stimulation, or so they thought. It was true, he had been dazed–frazzled–after his, what turned out to be his, final battle. But once he'd come to himself–he felt sure he'd come to himself–he knew he must say nothing. His master would come for him.

His final battle had been with The Wraith Dread Avenger of the Underworld.

His master's greatest enemy.

But his master was returning. He could feel it in his bones.

"HE'S COMING! HE'S COMING! OH, GODS–HE'S COMING!!!"

He screamed again. He spat and ground his teeth. He ran his feet up and down against the wall, tearing at the fabric with ragged, uncut toenails. It was happening, it was happening.

"HE'S COMING! HE'S COMING! HE'S CUH–"

Suddenly, as if a wire had been cut, he went silent. A pair of feet dropped clumsily to the floor. For the first time in ages, he lay perfectly still, ears cocked, listening.

"He's–he's here," he whispered softly.

After a moment, a key turned in the lock of the solid steel door that shut him away from the rest of the world. Slowly it creaked open, spreading white light into the dark room. The sudden illumination blinded him, and he instinctively ducked his head away. As he did, a group of shadows stepped inside.

Two immediately parted, moving to either side of the door-frame. One was shapely, the other grotesquely fat. Neither said anything but stood silent and straight, seemingly oblivious to anything around them–even each other.

Then, the third shadow swallowed up the entrance, blocking off the light itself. The black form was gigantic, ducking down to slip beneath the head jamb, turning sideways to move its immense frame past the sides. The massive figure held the primal power of the Kodiak bear, possessed the aura of a demigod come to life.

He gurgled and sucked in a deep breath. "Muh—Master..." he panted.

Heavy boots padded across the sodden fabric. A long regal cape covered massively powerful shoulders. A swarthy but handsome face of Middle-Eastern mien, triangular beard, blue-black and immaculate, stared down upon 416 with an intensity that seemed almost superhuman. Around the figure's right eye there seemed to be a peculiar marking. A red burn, a seared tattoo that seemed to form the image of a striking reptile.

"Hello, old friend. Magnus Khan," the Cobra said.

* * * * * *

The Cobra!

Few in the western world had seen him in the flesh, but every security agency in the world knew of him. He had once been the absolute ruler of Eritrea in Africa, known for his ferocity and rapacity for blood. His origins were a mystery. To the world at large he had simply appeared and, a few years later, disappeared. Nothing more could ever be ascertained.

His ideology was nonpolitical and nonreligious. His goal was the service of only himself. Yet, millions once bowed to him. Then, he had suddenly resurfaced, launching an all-out assault on Metro City that had leveled city blocks and wiped out thousands. He was supposed to have died three years ago, lost in a plunge from an airship hundreds of feet above the very city itself. The news of his demise caused celebrations in secret circles from the U.S. to North Korea. And, secretly, all blessed the name of the man who had stopped him. Word had gotten out that The Wraith had bested him.

Almost immediately after, the Cobra's servant and lover Natalya Blackova attempted a revenge that would have destroyed The Wraith and the United States itself. Incredibly, the Dread Avenger foiled that plot as well. In the struggle, Natalya had perished. The remnants of the Cobra's organization had gone on the run or committed suicide. At long last, the threat of the most dangerous man in the world was over.

The Cobra was dead. Everyone knew that. Everyone apparently except the man now looming majestically over Magnus Khan.

* * * * * *

He gazed down upon his former servant with an arched eyebrow. "It's been a long time," he commented almost mildly.

The pale, wide-eyed countenance of Magnus Khan stared slack-jawed upon his master. A line of spittle gently slipped down the corner of his lip. A slight giggle rasped between his teeth.

The Cobra surveyed the sight of his lackey. "Ah, Khan. Is this how I find you? How far you have fallen."

Magnus Khan rolled over upon his stomach. He wriggled forward like a crippled worm, reaching out a sallow cheek as if to rub it against the Cobra's ankle. With a snarl of anger the warlord pulled back his boot. Then it lashed out at the speed of light, straight into the pathetic underling's face.

Khan's neck jerked back so far it was amazing it didn't snap. Crimson fluid spurted hotly from his nose and lower jaw as the sickening sound of breaking bone and cartilage resounded through the cell.

"Do not touch me!" the Cobra growled. "You are not worthy of that!"

SERPENT RISING | 9

Magnus Khan retreated, yelping like a whipped pup. Bound as he was, he could do nothing to stop the flow of blood from his ruined jaw as bits of teeth fell from his mouth. Cringing against the wall, he howled in pain.

The Cobra snorted in disgust. Then he whipped around to face his two silent companions. Throughout the whole ordeal they had been waiting with frozen faces, unmoving. "Look at me!" the Cobra demanded.

Lydia and Jess raised their heads slightly, gazing into the Cobra's countenance. Suddenly, the white marble of the Cobra's own right orb came to incandescent light as he stared intently upon the two.

"You! Fat one, the one known as Jess," he barked toward the slovenly security guard. "Have you a weapon?"

His right eye gleamed brightly.

Jess's mouth sagged. A hammy hand hovered over his sidearm. "Yes...Master."

The Cobra pointed a gloved finger. "Then wait outside. Ensure we are not interrupted. Lethal force if required."

"Yes, Master." Jess turned on his chunky heel and stepped outside of the cell. He stopped upon the other side of the door and resumed his straight and stiff pose, hand resting upon the butt of his weapon.

The Cobra turned toward Lydia. "You may remain. I may have use for you later."

"Yes, Master," the entranced girl replied tonelessly. She did not react as the Cobra reached out beyond her to pull the door shut.

He then turned back to Magnus Khan, still cringing helplessly upon the floor. Khan shivered and drew back but could not tear his eyes away from his master's cold gaze.

The Cobra's demeanor was stern. "You were a man once, Khan," he pronounced quietly. "I made a man out of you.

What were you before me? Do you recall? A starving bandit leader, master of a ragged rabble, skulking for what you could find in the wastes of the Altai Mountains. Do you remember? That terrible winter, that zud so cold and bitter that every breath was torment and men died standing in their own footsteps? That was when we met. You charged at me upon your horse, hoping solely to steal my robe to warm yourself. I knocked you from the saddle and wrestled your steed to the ground before you could rise. Then I sliced the beast's neck and drank its warm blood before your very eyes."

Magnus Khan was silent now, pain seemingly forgotten. His eyes refused to tear themselves away from the giant before him.

"I would have left you to die where you lay. Your own men were too terrified to approach me. But I saw something in you—our eyes locked. A strength, a loyalty, a fealty. Someone whom I could shape in my own image and raise to my right hand. That was a great honor, my friend. One you soon recognized. I picked you up and we drank of your steed together. Then I took you and your men and pounded them into the first fruits of my great army. You were mighty then, Khan. I made you a warrior to be proud of. But now—look at you." The Cobra spat upon the floor as he regarded his former aide.

Then his countenance softened, slightly. "But I do not blame you for that. Not solely. I blame *him*. You served me well, Magnus Khan. I admit it. It was *he* who took you away from me. And not only you, but...." The Cobra's eyes clenched shut. Almost imperceptibly, the massive frame began to tremble. Softly at first, then with growing vigor, his face contorted in anger, his lips curled and twisted with unspoken fury. "Natalya." His voice trailed away.

SERPENT RISING | **11**

Then, as swiftly as it had come, the fury abated. The Cobra inhaled deeply, swallowed his anger, bringing his intense will to bear, and regained mastery of his emotions.

"Yes, *he* took you from me, my friend. Took you and so much more. And he shall pay for that. Oh, how he shall pay!"

The Cobra clenched his fist and for a moment he wondered whether he might actually lose himself in his fury. But, he quickly caught himself, and resolved to continue what he had started. He reached up, removed his cape, and spread it out upon the grimy floor. Then, he sat upon it, legs crossed, his eyes square upon Khan.

"Yes," the Cobra said. "My vengeance is near at hand. It will be swift and terrible. But first...there is a story to be told. You should feel honored, Magnus Khan. For never before has this tale been told in full to a living soul. Not even my Natalya knew it all. But...it is time for me to recall who and what I am, and how I came to be. I need to speak of this, to collect my thoughts and to strengthen myself for the great battle ahead. And to do that, I must tell it to someone. You are all I have left in this world." The Cobra leaned forward. "So, listen closely, my friend. For you, and you alone, shall hear words that have never passed these lips before and never shall again. Tonight you shall be privy to the origin...of the Cobra."

~ Chapter 2 ~

The Cobra shifted his position slightly, took a deep breath, and began to speak. "How old do I look, Khan? Have you never wondered at my appearance? Do I appear never-aging?" He sniffed. "In truth, I do not have all the answers myself. Am I immortal? At the very least, I appear to age *very* slowly." He stopped, rubbed his chin in consternation. "Does *he* do likewise, I wonder?"

After a time, he focused his gaze on Khan once again. "In truth, I have no need for immortality. My entrance into eternity is already ensured by the mark I shall leave upon mankind. When everything is accomplished, when all my plans unfold, whether I live a year after, a hundred, a thousand, is irrelevant. All that matters, in the end, is that everyone in the world from the most civilized country to the most primitive jungle tribe shall know that I was the greatest being that ever walked among them. That compared to me, all others were nothing. Alexander the Great, Attila, Napoleon, Hitler–nothing. Soon, very soon, every knee shall bow, and every tongue confess that the Cobra, and the Cobra alone, was truly...Master."

The Cobra sniffed, smirked at the sound of that, of his own supremacy. "But it has been a long road. Long and difficult. In the beginning, no one, let alone myself, would have begun to guess my destiny. The circumstances of my youth were humble, to say the least. I am Iranian by birth. Born during the reign of the last Shah. My full name is unimportant. I rejected it long ago. But I was known as Abdelkrim," he said, pausing briefly for effect.

"Do you know of it? It is the same as Abd el-Krim, the great Rif warlord. Perhaps that was Fate's means of hinting to me even then of my future glory. My birth, as I understand it, was quite rough. My mother nearly died in the delivery and there was some question as to whether I myself would survive. Yet, even then Fate played its hand in my favor. It would not allow me to perish. Somehow, I survived–even though I was puny and sickly, prone to every cough and cold that passed through the thin walls of our home. And I was undersized–half a head smaller than I should have been. I would be well into my adolescence before I experienced the growth spurt that made me as you see me now." He took a deep breath.

"My father was an ugly man. Inside and out. But he was canny enough to arrange a marriage to my mother, the daughter of one of Tehran's wealthiest families, and use their influence to obtain a high-ranking position in the Ministry of Finance. As to my mother herself–I have no memory of her. I asked my father about her once. All he did was beat me to the floor. But I found a photograph once. It showed the image of a very young and beautiful woman. A gentle woman. Compassionate. Undoubtedly, she would have loved me." He softened briefly, but only briefly.

"I am glad she died. A mother's love would only have weakened me. I needed the suffering I endured to harden my soul. This was in the sixties. My father's pre-eminence–his own words–ultimately came at a cost. His ambition, his lust for power, brought him under the Shah's glare. And the Shah was displeased. Only his *own* ambition could be permitted. So...my father lost everything: position, power, wealth. He was lucky to get away with his life. And, in the end, my mother. He killed her in a drunken rage when I was two. I believe he thought she was being untrue to him. At least that was the reason he gave. Father had cared only what she could do for him and once that was gone so was his interest in her. Regardless, afterwards, my father was forced to take me and relocate to a remote village on the borders of the Alborz Mountains. That was where I grew up. That was where I was tormented. Every single day of my life. Many was the indignity imposed upon my person. But I would not let them see me cry. Whatever happened, whatever they did to me, I always responded in the exact same fashion." His chest swelled at the memory. "I smiled."

* * * * * *

IRAN - MANY YEARS EARLIER

"Goosaleh! Goosaleh! Stupid little goosaleye goh! Are you going to cry, goosaleye goh?"

Seven boys, perhaps no older than ten, surrounded another of similar age. Two held the central one tightly by the arms. In front one boy, bigger and burlier than the rest, held a fist clutching tiny brown balls–goat droppings–while yet another boy jerked back the central lad's head, forcing his mouth open.

A cruel sight, but not an unusual one. Bullies waging war against a smaller child was a worldwide phenomenon. But there was a crucial difference between this scene and so many similar ones replicated across the planet. In most of those, the younger, weaker child would probably be crying.

This one smiled.

The boy was painfully pale and thin, a good half head smaller than others his age. His name was Abdelkrim. As the other boys roughhoused him, the corners of his lips curled upward at each taunt and punch directed his way.

He smiled. He did not cry. Even at that young age, he refused to give them that satisfaction. He gazed steadily at the leader of the gang accosting him. That boy, Agrin, was as squat and burly as Abdlekrim was small and slight. He held the handful of droppings right before Abdelkrim's eyes, grinning triumphantly.

Abdelkrim struggled valiantly but unsuccessfully. He never stopped smiling. Hooting raucously, Agrin opened his hand, dropping the dried pebbles down the smaller boy's mouth, forcing him to gulp them down. It was the most disgusting thing Abdelkrim had ever swallowed. But, as usual, his face did not show his distaste.

He smiled.

Abdelkrim always smiled. Though his eyes were purpled, and his lip was swollen, he would not cry. No. He would never let them see him cry.

Which only made his enemies even madder.

"Stupid piece of dog—" Agrin snarled in frustration, striking Abdelkrim in the face with a sharp, bony fist. "You *like* this? Start crying! Cry, damn you—cry!"

Abdelkrim made no reply. He just stood there.

Smiling.

The bigger boy roared with fury and seized Abdelkrim by the shirt, throwing him to the earth. The dust and grime tasted little better than the goat droppings. Abdelkrim could not keep back a cough. In response, Agrin ground his face deeper into the dirt.

"Cry!" Agrin demanded.

Abdelkrim did not. He rolled over onto his back, gazing up at his tormentor.

Grinning.

Agrin kicked him hard in the side. "You stupid lashy! I'll kill you if you don't cry! You hear me? I'll kill you!"

One of the other boys reached out and stopped Agrin before he could strike any further. He was tired of the game. "Let's go," he said. "This isn't fun anymore. The kussi's too damn stupid to even know when to cry. Let's go play football."

Agrin paused, his eyes narrowed. But he stepped away. "Fine," he said, leaning over to send a wad of spit into Abdelkrim's face. "Go home, kussi. You're not wanted here." He turned away, the rest of the mob went with him. A few moments later Abdelkrim was alone, lying supine in the dusty street.

He lay there for a long time. Then, he reached up and wiped the mucus from his face. He rolled over and spat several times, trying to get the taste of feces and soil from his mouth. The smile faded from his bruised lips and his gorge rose.

But he would not cry. Never would he cry.

Painfully, he struggled to his feet. Off in the distance he could hear laughter and a ball being kicked about. He glanced toward the shacks surrounding him that served as homes for the townspeople. No sympathetic eyes peered through windows into his, no welcoming arms offered him comfort or succor. If any had witnessed Agrin and his thugs beating him, not one had cared. He was Abdelkrim, son of the most despised man in the village. The scion of a drunkard and traitor who had worked against their beloved and revered Shah. Or at least that was what the Shah had wanted–forced?–everyone to think. That was his new reality. That's the way it would always be.

Abdelkrim sighed to himself. Then, limping a bit, he slowly began making his way home. To Abdelkrim, home was a hastily-cobbled together collection of timber boards, listing and unpainted, that made the ramshackle huts of the rest of the village seem like luxury mansions by comparison. No one remembered who had built it or why. It had been abandoned for years, the locals utilized it as the local rubbish dump, until Abdelkrim's father arrived. Since the villagers had left everything they hated there to rot, they figured he could rot there as well. His money and influence gone, his dignity torn to shreds, Abdelkrim's father had had no choice but to accept it as the new home for himself and his boy.

A ragged sheet served as a makeshift door, and Abdelkrim pulled it aside to enter. As he did, he held his breath. With any luck his father wouldn't be drunk that afternoon. He should have known better. Where the old man found the liquor, Abdelkrim could not begin to guess. But his father was never without a bottle somehow. The old man wheeled at the sound of his son coming in and greeted him with his usual candor. "By Allah! Have you been fighting again?"

Abdelkrim sighed but said nothing. There was no point. Even though he had not himself thrown so much as a punch, all his father would see through his blurred vision was his son's bruised eyes and bloody lip.

Looking at him, Abdelkrim reflected that his father was, indeed, an ugly little man. Fat and squat and mottled, with a flabby, wide-mouthed face. He resembled nothing so much as a repulsive toad that had somehow reared up upon its hind legs and decided to remain there. In one of his hands was clutched a bottle of imported American whisky.

"Didn't I tell you not to go out picking fights anymore?" the drunken man howled. "What do I have to do to get you to listen...hit you myself?" Which he did.

The blow wasn't much harder, really, than one of Agrin's punches. But it was the reeking blast of booze upon his father's breath that made the boy jerk his head back automatically. That was a stupid move and Abdelkrim knew it. Any reaction, real or imagined, to his father's discipline only enraged the old man further. The blow came again and this time Abdelkrim found himself down upon the packed earth that served as the hovel's floor, his cheek red and stinging.

Father lifted the bottle and sent a geyser of liquid down his throat. "Weak, stupid little koonie," he snarled. "That's what you are. Weak and stupid. Is that what you're going to be all your life, boy? A stupid little koonie? Or are you going to become a real man like me? I was *somebody,* once, until my enemies stabbed me in the back. But I'm going to be somebody again, boy. Just you wait. One day, they'll all pay." A green glob of sputum hit the floor. Abdelkim's father wiped his mouth on his arm, glared once again down at his son. "They'll all pay."

They'll all pay.

The words rang through Abdelkrim's head. He saw his father hovering above, still furious. The youth did not rise, did not make any move. It was not the first time he had heard those words of his sire.

They'll all pay.

But this time there was something different about them. Abdelkrim could not explain it, but it was as if he truly *heard* them for the first time. Heard and realized just what they meant. As he lay there it seemed as if the scene above him was suddenly pulled aside, like a curtain yanked away from a window. His father, bleary-eyed and listing, faded away to nothing.

Abdelkrim found himself standing in the center of his nameless village, alone in the night. Even the moon was hidden behind a cloud. The street was dark and empty. It was as though no change had fallen upon the homes of the village about him, yet Abdelkrim somehow knew years had passed since he had walked the street that very morning.

From the shadows, someone approached. Abdelkrim tensed, felt a sudden surge of fear, but was unable to tear his eyes away from the nearing silhouette. It came forward, closer and closer, until the moon slipped from behind its veil to reveal the shambling approach of an outrageously thin and scrawny figure, more living scarecrow than human being. It shuffled right up to and past him, apparently unaware of his presence. Yet with a shock, Abdelkrim recognized the figure that lurched by—recognized him as surely as he would recognize his own reflection in the mirror. It was *himself*—Abdelkrim as an adult. An adult much older, scraggly and malnourished, clothed in rags.

The figure tottered slightly as he walked, and Abdelkrim realized that he, this future vision of himself, was as inebriated as his father was now. Then the drunken figure staggered, stumbled, and fell in the very spot that Agrin had slammed him, the younger Abdelkrim, onto earlier that day. And then there was Agrin himself, as squat and burly an adult as he was a child, standing beside this fallen figure to kick him hard between the ribs.

"Koonie! Koonie! Drunk goosaleye goh! Just like your old man! What good are you save for me to kick? Stupid drunk koonie!"

The older Abdelkrim smiled. But not to show his tormentors that all the invective they could spill upon him was beneath him. This was a sign of joy. With a thrill of horror, Abdelkrim realized this wretched, sodden version of himself *liked* what was happening. It proved to him that he was alive, showed that someone was paying attention to him.

The young Abdlekrim felt sicker at the sight than any goat droppings could make him. Then, as he watched, the scene grew blurry, faded into murky hues like a fresh watercolor in the rain. Replacing it was a fresh scene. Now it seemed to Abdelkrim as if he were hovering high in the sky, over a massive palace the beauty and grandeur the likes of which he had never imagined. A massive thing of blazing white marble, its borders stretching for miles as far as his eyes could see. The gates were of solid gold, the walls embedded with fist-sized gemstones of diamond and emerald and onyx. The mightiest king could never dream of possessing such an edifice.

The courtyard was filled wall to wall with men and women, children and elders, of every age and color and ethnicity. Like the previous vision–for what else could it be?– none seemed to take any notice of his arrival. Rather, all were gazing with a worshipful intentness toward one balcony that stretched out stories above them all over the yard.

The crowd was eerily silent, breathless with anticipation. Abdelkrim could only wonder whom they were waiting for. An emperor? He would have to be an emperor, indeed, to command such a diverse crowd.

Then, as it seemed to catch its breath in unison, the crowd all dropped instantly to its knees. A figure appeared upon the balcony, and the crowd instantly plunged their faces in utter obeisance to the ground.

"HAIL!" they cried out, boy and girl and man and woman, "WE HAIL YOU, GREAT ONE! WE WHO ARE ABOUT TO DIE SALUTE YOU!!!"

Abdelkrim looked up toward the balcony—and gasped. There, standing in lordly majesty on its lofty heights, gazing down upon the world with a cold disdain that bespoke of his utter control of it—was *himself*. But not the filthy scarecrow of before. This version of himself was a towering giant, an immense figure of height and broad muscle, caressed in a silken cape that flowed over powerful shoulders. His beard was short and triangular, and the face...the face was the strongest, most dominating countenance he had ever seen. And it was *his* face, *his* countenance.

The adult Abdelkrim did not speak. He indicated the crowd should rise. As one they did, but none raised their eyes to meet his. Abdelkrim then realized: all these people, young and old, rich and poor, had but one thought—to serve the one above who was master of them all. He—the future him?—ruled every one of these people completely, utterly, with an authority that could not be denied. If he declared that, as one, they should slay themselves before him, not one would hesitate.

Looming over the waiting crowd, the adult Abdelkrim raised one hand, palm flat. Then, as the young one watched, he swung out his arm and...

"Boy! Are you listening to me?"

As swiftly as it came, the vision vanished. Abdelkrim was left staring at the bloated, furious face of his father. The old man had yanked him up from the floor.

"Get up!" he snarled. "Don't just lie there like a dog. Lazy pig. Listen to me." He raised his hand to slap the boy again.

Abdelkrim looked at him. Looked at the flushed-crimson face and blood-soaked eyes. He thought about how much he despised him. He thought of Agrin and the other villagers, about how much he despised them as well. The truth hit him like a bolt from the heavens. Something—Allah, the Fates, *something*—had just given him a choice. He had two roads, two destinies to choose from. What he did now would lead inevitably toward one or the other. That choice was his to make, that very instant. One, a life of misery and horror as he slowly destroyed himself as his father destroyed his own life. The other...

Abdelkrim knew he could not wait a second longer. He made his decision. "Rattaeepiwigp," he said.

His father blinked. "What?"

"Rattaeepwiapg," Abdelkrim spat again between his teeth.

His old man snarled and shook him. "What the hell did you just say? Repeat it. Say it clearly."

Abdelkrim paused and took a deep breath. He met his father's eyes very carefully. Then he smiled. "I said," he enunciated slowly, "that I would rather have sex with a pig than hear another word you say."

His father's roar must have been heard clear to the other end of the village. As must have the crashing of the bottle over Abdelkrim's head, sending rivulets of glass and booze and blood coursing down over his ears.

Then the old man was upon him, hurling him once more to the earthen floor, pounding fists into the boy's face and gut again and again and again. Abdelkrim clenched his teeth. Another wave of nausea welled up in his stomach and before he could stop it, he vomited, right over himself and his father. The bile further fueled the old man's rage. He grabbed his son's head and slammed it into the ground. "How dare you? How *dare* you?"

Abdelkrim could no longer see out of his right eye. The left saw everything through a blood-scarlet haze. His ears could only hear the frenzied pounding of his heart. But he smiled. He *smiled.*

That was the last his father could stand. With a final howl, he yanked the boy to his feet, dragged him toward the curtained door of the hut. "Get out! GET OUT!"

Twisting Abdelkrim's arms behind his back, the elder man physically thrust him outside into a pile of debris. "You are no longer my son, do you hear? This is no longer your home. You are nothing. Nothing but a filthy animal. Now get out of here! GET OUT!" Abdelkrim's father wheeled and reentered the hut. The ragged sheet flapped shut, edges swaying from the motion.

Outside, the remnants of the bottle clung to the sodden strings of Abdelkrim's hair. Blood trickled from cuts in his scalp. His eyes were swollen beyond black and his lips felt thick and blood soaked. He smelt of rubbish, vomit and cheap liquor. Yet, for the first time in his life, he felt energized. Alive. Something had happened to him. Something...incredible. He had seen the two paths his future could take. In the first, he became as drunk and powerless as his father. In that vision, the world slapped him, and he loved it. In the second...he had slapped the world, and it loved *him* for it.

Carefully, wiping away the grime and blood, young Abdelkrim lifted himself to his feet. He gazed over the hut that had been the only home he had known, toward the mountains just beyond. In the distance he could see the snow-capped peak of Damavand, the highest mountain in the country. It seemed to him it was looking back at him, calling him.

I'm waiting, boy. Waiting for your next move.

Abdelkrim still hesitated. He knew what he must do now, but could not fathom the means. How was he to find food? Water? How was he to survive the coldness of the night? If he did as the mountain beckoned him to do, surely, he would be dooming himself to a slow, lingering death.

No, boy, Damavand seemed to say. *You will be taking the first step to your destiny.*

Abdelkrim nodded in reply. Damavand would be heeded. Slowly, for he still limped from his previous beating, he turned his back upon his father's hut and the dusty village. One day, he sensed, he would return. But for now, he had other places to be. He passed beneath the great mass of stony sentinels that surrounded him, becoming swallowed up in shadow. If it were the shade of the mountains or the darkness of his own soul, he could not say. Only one thing rang through his head now as he passed on to the greatness he knew awaited him.

Someday, they'll all pay.

~ Chapter 3 ~

"**A**nd thus, I left my father, my village, and my former life behind. To this day I do not regret it," the Cobra related to his erstwhile lackey. "I am not Muslim, any more than I am a follower of Christ. In the end, I worship only myself. The Roman Catholic cosmology of the afterlife makes an excellent representation of what I would experience over the next few years. For the first decade of my life, I had experienced Hell. Then I saw a vision of Heaven calling out to me. But to get there, I needed purification. The wilderness of the Alborz Mountains would become my Purgatory." He bowed his head as the memories flowed.

"Master...the Alborz," Khan sputtered.

"Yes, Khan. You have been to the Alborz, but you do not know them, my friend. They are chameleons. Each side presents a different face from the other. The northern slopes, facing the Caspian, are green and verdant, watered by cool brooks and shaded with the leaves of beech and oak and hornbeam. The southern slopes, blocked from the breezes of the sea, are the exact opposite. Here the land is barren and lifeless. Water is hard to find, and what foliage there is offers no protection from the heat of the sun. This was where I would spend my next ten years. But only a few days after I left, I wondered if I would ever survive that long. I had thought I knew hunger and thirst in the hovel I had called home. That was nothing. By my fourth day in the wilderness, I was panting for the slightest bit of moisture to cool my tongue. The groans of my belly at home had been but minor murmurs compared to the howls of famine that came to me now."

Khan murmured something indecipherable. The Cobra raised his head, his eyes focused intently on his former lackey, before continuing. "My feet were blistered and bloody. Each step was an agony of bruises and blisters. My skin a scarlet cake of cracked skin. I froze during the nights and baked as in an oven by day. And nowhere could I find succor. As I lay myself down to sleep each night, I wondered if I would be rising to the next morn. Yet I welcomed the pain eagerly. As my body weakened, my spirit and will to survive grew stronger. And on the tenth day, the Fates sent me something that told me I was upon the right path."

"Bah...bah..." Khan mumbled.

"My first friend, Khan."

* * * * * *

IRAN - MANY YEARS EARLIER

The sun's rays beat down like invisible hammers fresh from the forge, but Abdelkrim walked on. Large, fang-tailed scorpions, their venom-arcs at the ready, skittered from rock and arid bush as he passed, but he ignored them, and they did not strike. The high, stolid stone of Damavand seemed to grow no closer, yet still he walked. As he turned to gaze wistfully in the direction he had come, he saw prints of blood left behind in the caked earth. But, Abdelkrim marched inexorably on.

And he smiled.

He smiled at the elements that threatened to beat him down just as he did to Agrin, his father, and all his other tormentors. He smiled to show them he would never bend. Never break. He smiled to spite them all, now and forevermore.

But sun and wind cannot be offended by smiles. Hunger and thirst are the most callous of insults. And rest there must be for all that called itself man. Finally, even Abdelkrim had to pause, rest his weakened body against one of the many hot, scraping boulders fallen loose and rough among the inclines of the surrounding hills, and try to ease his weary limbs. He glanced upwards.

Besides the scorpions, the vultures had been the only living beasts he had seen for days, their sinister black forms arcing expectantly high above. They hoped there would soon be a fresh meal to sate their hunger. Abdelkrim did not waste time to show them what he thought of them. Yet he knew he would die if he could not find water and shelter soon. The problem was, other than walking about aimlessly, he had no idea how to find them. Perhaps the vultures would have their meal after all.

For a moment he wondered if he had dreamed the whole thing, if his vision of the future had been nothing more than mere fancy or, worse still, the evil emanations of some demon or spirit out to lure him to this place of death.

Abdelkrim did not believe in demons, djinns or other such beings. But now he mused if he might be wrong.

He took a long breath, the hot air burning his lungs. Then he thrust himself off the boulder and began walking again. A delusion? A trap? Then so be it. Better he should perish here, alone and savaged by the elements than return home and slowly become that pathetic wretch he had seen in his first vision. Real or not, he would gladly die before becoming such a creature.

The sun lashed its heat down as the nightmarish beasts swirled above. There seemed to be nothing else to do but go on. It was only coincidence that he lifted his head to regard the gray mountain slopes surrounding him.

That was when he saw it.

It was the merest chink within the rocks. A thin slice of blackness ripped jaggedly through the slate above. A shadow deep back amid the stones and so narrow it could not be seen without the light falling just so. Without that light, Abdelkrim would have staggered past, never knowing it was there. It might be nothing more than a tiny hollow only a few inches deep worn into the rocks from wind and sun, but it was an offering of shelter, however little, and Abdelkrim needed that shelter. He could rest no longer without some protection from the searing heat of the day and bitter cold of the night. Swiftly, he scrambled up the pebbly earth towards it, thrusting his exhaustion aside. More than once he slipped, injuring knee and elbow, but he refused to give up so close to his goal.

Without hesitation, upon reaching the cleft, he squeezed himself in. It was a tight fit even for his scrawny, malnourished frame. Raw red flesh scraped sharply against the serrated stone edges. But even as it did, the cleft widened out into a grand, cool blackness even Abdelkrim had not expected. This was no mere chink carved into the rock. This was a fully fledged cave.

The beams of sunlight reached only a few feet inside, forming a shaft of illumination that barely penetrated the depth of the cavern. Beyond that, he could see nothing, though he felt, instinctively, that the cave extended much further than he could immediately sense. Abdelkrim stepped carefully further within. For a moment he welcomed the sudden lowering of temperature about him. It felt at least ten degrees cooler than outside. As his eyes slowly adjusted to what light there was just inside the entrance, he cocked his ears to listen for any sound.

Drip.

Abdelkrim's eyes widened, and he listened even more closely. He hardly dared breathe lest it drown out what he thought he had heard.

Drip-drip-drip.

His ears had not lied. It was the sound of water. Somewhere in this cave was life giving elixir. Abdelkrim had to find it. He took a deep breath, then plunged past the shaft of light into the black interior.

For a long moment he could neither see nor sense anything. Even the slow, precious tone of the drips eluded him. Abdelkrim strained his ears, desperately.

Drip-drip-drip.

There! Now, if he could just find the source...

Slowly, patiently, he moved cautiously deeper into the midnight void, each step careful and deliberate. No other sound, save for the elusive dripping of water and his soft footfalls, could be heard. His eyes finally started to adjust to the darkness, but he yearned for a torch to help guide his path.

Drip-drip-drip.

The sound grew louder, more discernible. Abdelkrim's feet crunched beneath what must have been centuries of fill. Several times he tapped against small stalagmites. The illuminated entrance behind him shrank to a tiny halo seemingly miles away. It didn't matter. The water was close now, so very close.

And suddenly, his sandaled feet felt cold and damp. The sound of the drips grew louder. Dropping to his knees, Abdelkrim reached out, plunged his hands into a deep chill. He had found it. An underground pool or stream.

It was his initial instinct to plunge into the cooling liquid, to bathe and drink to excess, at his leisure. But he knew this to be unhealthy, and therefore, unwise. He would rest awhile here, he decided, refresh himself bit by bit until he had regained his strength. Then, he would have to consider finding food. How he would go about that he did not yet know. First things first, however...

It was then that he heard the growl.

It came from the shadows somewhere off to Abdelkrim's left, low and fierce. He whipped around toward it, just in time to see a flash of two tiny emerald eyes in the inky void. They glinted with a savage ferocity.

In his quest–his incredible thirst–for water, he had failed to consider someone, or something, else might be sharing the cave with him. The hairs on the back of his neck sprang upright. He could hear and feel its warm breath now—and that breath was coming closer. Swiftly, his hands darted about in the gloom, seeking something, anything, he could use as a potential weapon. He reached out—and snatched his hand back with an involuntary yelp as his hand touched something sharp, drawing blood upon his palm. Automatically he found himself sucking at the wound even as the growl came again...his invisible stalker had sensed the blood. Abdelkrim realized whatever had cut him was the weapon he'd been seeking—and he thrust out his hand again, curling it around what proved to be a stalagmite. A quick examination with his hand showed the top was as tipped and sharp as the head of a spear. He yanked, hard, and it broke off from the cave floor into his hand—a makeshift earthen dagger. He hoped it would be enough.

A movement in the dark and the glitter of emerald again. Small and low to the floor. Abdelkrim crinkled his nose and a distinct feline scent reached his nostrils. He instantly realized what he was facing. A leopard. The Persian leopard, still common in the mountains though becoming rarer as they were slowly being exterminated. Abdelkrim clenched his weapon tightly. The emeralds cautiously slunk closer. Realistically, he knew he stood little chance against such a predator. But in the close confines of the cave...perhaps there *was* a chance. Once more, the remembrance of his vision flashed before his eyes. If he survived, he would do everything in his power to make that vision a reality. His destiny would not be denied now. If not, he would fall beneath the beast's claws fighting like the lord he might have become.

Enough waiting. If he was to strike, he must strike now. With a scream of defiance, Abdelkrim darted toward the gleams of green, slicing out with his stone knife. The tiny emeralds flashed away back into the black. Abdelkrim's arm flailed through the air, striking nothing. The creature had clearly dodged out of his way. He froze, waiting to feel the great weight of the cat upon him, of its claws rending the flesh from his bones.

Nothing happened. For a long moment, all was silent. He now saw no sign of those green eyes. But he heard the rustle of something in the dark, moving, it seemed, deeper into the interior of the mountain. Was the beast fleeing?

He didn't know why, but Abdelkrim found himself following. In a minute, he could discern the soft pad of paws upon the cave floor before him. They didn't seem particularly hurried or fearful. Abdelkrim went on but kept a firm grip upon his only weapon. The cave soon opened up into an expansive subterranean lair. Slivers of light streaked down from slits in the roof, letting in beads of sunlight flitting in this direction and that. Then, the leopard retreated into just such a sliver, and its true form came into focus.

Abdelkrim stopped dead, blinking. His would-be stalker was, indeed, a leopard. But not the leopard he was expecting. The creature gazing at him calmly, fearlessly, with a low growl rumbling in its throat, was little more than a cub. Certainly not fully grown as best as Abdelkrim could tell. Its spots had not quite yet come in, and its eyes were bright green in hue. Yet it was large for its age. And now proved quite unafraid of the human it faced, for it gazed intensely and coolly upon Abdelkrim, utterly unharmed and undeterred by his earlier failed attack. It sat upon its haunches, watching for a moment. Then, casually, it raised itself up upon all fours and trotted toward him with nary a sign of fear or menace.

Abdelkrim tensed as it did, for he suspected the cub was too young to have left its mother. That meant she was likely nearby, full-grown and undoubtedly anxious to locate its wayward child. There could be other cubs, too, that it would seek to protect. This cave would be a perfect den for them. He should have known better than to come there. He had been desperate to survive. But now...?

The cub padded onward, not pausing until it stopped directly in front of him. Abdelkrim gazed down at it. It gazed up at him. Brown and emerald eyes met and held the other in a timeless moment. Then, it slipped between Abdelkrim's legs, swiveled around, and started further back into the cave.

After a few paces it stopped and turned its head to look back at him. It seemed to be urging him to follow. Abdelkrim hesitated. The beast could be leading him straight into its mother's fangs. And yet—whatever had been guiding his steps thus far had not been proven wrong. He still did not believe in any god, but perhaps, just perhaps, there truly was such a thing as fate. As destiny. And for the moment, destiny was telling him to follow the cub. Abdelkrim nodded. So be it.

His eyes met the leopard's again, and he gave the beast a silent command to wait. His eyes darted around, searching for another, perhaps deadlier, weapon. The cave floor was strewn with dry stems and branches from some bush outside. And...was that some flint over there? It was. Luck? No...destiny!

Swiftly, he curled the stems around the top of his stalagmite weapon, then set at work upon the flint. He clacked the rocks together several times until they sparked. Quickly, he pressed the yellowed plants to the sparks and set them alight. A makeshift torch. It would not last long, but it would suffice long enough to light his way—or serve as another defense if worse came to worse. Then the cat began moving. Abdelkrim followed. They came to and passed another, smaller pool, and descended further into the deeper recesses of the cavern. A few dozen more steps, and the leopard stopped. Abdelkrim could now see why its mother had not defended it.

The body lay cold and stiff upon the cavern floor. At its side lay two more bodies, much tinier and grayer. The young leopard moved up against the corpse of its mother, rubbing gently against it, and then looked back up at Abdelkrim. It gazed at him expectantly. Still holding the torch, Abdelkrim went to his knees. Placing the torch carefully to one side, he reached out a hand cautiously toward the leopard. He made no cute sounds, he simply held out a hand. The cat ducked its head beneath his fingers. After a moment, it began to purr. And emerald eyes looked straight once again into Abdelkrim's own.

In that instant, Abdelkrim understood. Like him, this creature was motherless, rejected. But determined, against all odds, to survive. Abdelkrim ran his hand gently down the leopard's body. It arched its back beneath his ministrations. Then it drew back, looked over at what had been its mother, and back at Abdelkrim. He heard another growl, but this time not from the cat's throat. He himself was growling.

Abdelkrim smiled and picked his torch back up. Very soon it would extinguish, but that was all right. He knew where the water was, which would sustain him for some time. And food? He was hungry, that was true, but he was now so resolute as to his future, that it mattered little to him in that moment. He knew–*knew*–he would find food, and soon.

It was his destiny.

* * * * * *

The Cobra sat pensively in the cell, staring silently for a moment before continuing his narrative. "That day Pashmir—as I named him—and I forged a bond that could not, would not, be broken by anything save death itself. At long last, I had found a soul akin to my own. On the outside, seemingly puny and worthless, but within—a storm of thunder and fire, determined to survive no matter what the cost. Even from that day we were more than simply master and beast–we were brothers. Now we had to learn to survive."

Khan sat upright, remaining silent, but jittery, then began to sway to and fro on his bed.

"The cave gave us shelter and water," the Cobra continued, "but we needed food. Destiny alone could only fill our bellies for so long. So, if we were to live—we had to learn to kill."

Khan stood, and began to silently pace the room.

"We started with mice and rats," the Cobra said. "Then hares and conies. I shaped knives out of flint. Later, through much trial and error, I learned to make spears out of my knives and such wood I could find in that sparse environment. More practice, and I fashioned myself a crude bow and several arrows. I practiced with them until I could strike a rabbit's eye at a dozen paces. Meanwhile, Pashmir learned to walk with a silent pad, to stalk our prey like a whisper of wind, to wait until I gave the sign to feed.

"M...m..." Khan muttered under his breath, but the Cobra gave him no heed.

"It was not easy, that first year or so. We stumbled, we erred. Like most wild predators, we failed more often than we succeeded. Many was the night we fell asleep to the rumbling of our stomachs. But we persisted. We persevered. Pashmir and I shared one thing—the determination to survive at all costs. We would not give in to death. We simply would not.

"But...master..." Khan mumbled again, whether he meant to interrupt, whether he actually had something meaningful to say, the Cobra knew not. Nor did he care.

"Silence, lackey! You may not speak now." He took a deep breath before continuing once again. "For years we stalked the wilderness together. We avoided all men we saw, bandits and shepherds and errant wanderers alike, keeping to the wildest places where the growing modernization of the outside world would not come. And, as you can see—we changed. Changed enormously. They were the greatest years of my life. I say that with all honesty. Despite all the hardships, all the dangers—for the first time I could truly say

I was happy. When your greatest care is what you are going to eat that day, all else fades into insignificance. For the longest time I wanted to do nothing else but roam the wilderness with my brother. The vision that had moved me to that point seemed to fade more and more as the years went by. I'm ashamed to admit it." He bowed his head with regret. "But it never deserted me. Not for a moment. It paled, it cooled, yet it never took flight from me. I believe, looking back, that it needed to fade for a while, in order for me to concentrate on survival first. To increase my strength, my will. To learn the skills I needed that would ultimately lead me to my destiny. Truly, if I had not hardened myself in the wilderness as I did, I would not be here before you now. My future chose to step aside for a time, to test and purify me.

Khan sputtered some more gibberish before ceasing at a stern gesture from his master.

"But it could not stay away forever. Little by little, I felt its siren call, crying out to me in my dreams. I shut it out, briefly ignored it, tamped it down into the deep recesses of my memory. But ultimately my vision would not be silenced. Ever louder and more persistent it called to me, day by day and night by night, until at last I realized I had no choice but to put this idyllic life aside and once again take up the path toward my destiny. Then one night, in the depths of sleep, it returned, stronger and clearer than ever before. It must have disturbed me, for I felt Pashmir stir as he lay at my feet, and he gazed at me as I awoke. But he made no protest as I rose and put out the remains of our small fire. It was still late in the night, but when I gestured for him to follow, he came without hesitation. As if he knew something great was about to happen.

"Master...master..."

The Cobra stopped and stared harshly at Khan. He would brook no more interruptions. "I had learned what I needed to know there in that wilderness. Now I had other lessons to master. Lessons that would enable me to be master of the entire world. But there was something else I had to do first."

~ Chapter 4 ~

IRAN - MANY YEARS EARLIER

The night echoed with laughter. The sound of mirth carried over the ramshackle hovels, passed through wooden shutters and doors, reaching the ears of all who lived there. Listening, the people shuddered and huddled even deeper beneath their rough, thin blankets. The laughter that rang out under the stars was not ordinarily the high-pitched merriment of innocent children, nor the gay, familiar amusement of old and dear friends, or, indeed, of any man, woman or child. It was the chortle of the desert hyena, raucous and malicious. It was the whine of the jackal, cruel and gloating. It was the sound of evil on wings.

Hyena and jackal, however, would be offended to hear they were being compared to the actual makers of such exhilaration that night. The laughter came from beasts indeed, but of the two-legged variety. Man. Only they were capable of taking such joy in the goings-on at that moment. Even the desert predators held more dignity and honor in their mangy souls than did those fools.

The moon was full but not bright, laying low in the sky that late autumn night. Shadows pasted themselves to the edges of the light. The air was heavy with an invisible blanket of frost, bitterly woven with threads of ice crystals and polar wind. The mountains appeared like jagged white fingers, clawing to pierce the sickly winter orb above. A perfect night for evil.

The laughter rang out again, hoarse and cawing. The two-legged beasts were enjoying themselves immensely tonight. There were six of them all told, hanging about a rubbish fire sparked in the empty lea of packed earth the villagers called their Square. They were young men, scarcely into their twenties. Yet these six absolutely dominated the lives of the rest of the inhabitants. Abdelkrim knew them well.

All were big men, burly and strong. They were fast with their fists and faster with their blades if any villager opposed their will. As children they had been bullies. As adults they were professional thugs. Four were standing, two others lounged lazily upon the rough stone circle that bordered the village well. Compared to the rest, these two seemed positively lackadaisical. They took no part in the roistering, preferring instead to take deep, slow draws from black, long-handled pipes clenched in their mouths. The wisps of smoke floating skyward from those stems were thick and heavy, strangely potent in their scent, like too much incense poured into a basin.

Opium. The two were lost in a drug-induced haze.

The other four paid no attention to them. The fire roared as a couple of the men threw more trash onto it. The laughter picked up again, grew crueler. All their scrutiny was upon what appeared to be a large black bundle rolled up on the ground between them. A low, despairing moan escaped from it, proving it was actually no bundle at all. The largest and burliest of the men shot out a foot to kick it. "Shut up," the man snarled. "Stupid little bitch. Think you're too good for us? Ignored me when I tried to speak to you at the market in Tehran? Gendeh! Now you're going to pay for your stuck-up airs."

The bundle that was not a bundle rolled painfully over—to reveal a pair of fabric a pair of large and reddened eyes brimming with tears of fear and shame. "Please!" the girl in the burqa begged. "Let me go!"

"What do you think, Agrin?" one of the thugs asked with mock concern. "Should we take her home? Leave her alone?"

"After we're done with her, Bijan," Agrin leered lecherously. "I want to teach her a little lesson about ignoring men first."

"You are not my father! You are not my brother! The Law of the Prophet demands I not speak to—"

"I don't care!" Agrin, once leader of a gang of village children and now leader of a similar band of adults, glared down at the girl he had snatched off the streets of their village. "Good little Islamic girl. 'Oh, I would *never* speak to a male stranger! It's against the law.' Arrogant cow! What have you been doing all these years, waiting for Papa to pick you a proper husband? Well, I'm going to be your husband tonight. We all are. Then we're going to take you back home and have a good laugh when your precious Papa and brother see what's been done to you and decide to kill you to defend their family honor. That's part of the law, too, you know. Killing a woman who's been used by a man. It's *her* fault,

SERPENT RISING | **41**

you see. If she were a *good* girl, she never would have been raped in the first place!"

"Please, let me go! My father is wealthy, he can—"

Agrin kicked her once more. "Shut up! Strip her, Babak."

"Wait, Agrin!" Bijan suddenly cried, racing over to one of the loungers at the well, neither of whom seemed to have taken any notice of what was happening just a few feet away. He yanked a pipe out of one of their mouths, ignoring the smoker's sudden, albeit sullen protests. "Give her a good whiff of this. Have her be an addict when we drop her off at her door. Besides, it'll make her easier to handle."

Agrin shook his head. "I'm not wasting any opium on her. We grow the stuff for ourselves, not anyone else. I *want* her to know what's going on." He nodded to Babak, who hauled the girl to her feet. Grinning lustfully, the group began their vile task.

That's when more laughter rang out. More laughter, but a kind totally unlike the hooting guffaws of the young thugs. This sound that seemed to come from everywhere in the darkness surrounding the fire was a different thing. It was deeper, more controlled. It rolled forth like a distant thunder on the wind, filling up their surrounds and enveloping the shadows. Like their own braying cacophony, there was a sense of cruelty to it, a sensation of malice. But a malice directed toward *them* rather than to the girl.

The thugs looked about in the darkness for the source. They could see no one. The laughter continued a moment, and then a voice as deep as the laughter called out. "Oh, Agrin, Agrin. You haven't changed in the least. Still a brute at heart. Still a fool."

Agrin's eyes widened. "Who said that?"

The voice did not answer.

"Who said that?" Agrin demanded again, gazing around him. "No one speaks to me that way. Come out. I know everyone in this village. I'll find out who you are."

"But you *do* know me, Agrin. You all do. Every day for five years you dared to rub my face in the dust of this village. You beat me until I was black and blue. And every time you did—I smiled."

Agrin blinked. "Smiled? It can't be—" A pause of surprise, then he threw his head back and laughed. "Abdelkrim! Fellows, our little goosaleh has come back. Son of the village drunkard. Cowering in the shadows as always. Ha! Didn't die out in the mountains, little goosaleh goh? Come back to let us beat you again? Ha! Was your father happy to see you, or was he sober enough to even notice?"

For a long moment there was silence in the darkness. "See for yourself," Abdelkrim ultimately said.

Something swished in the air and suddenly a thick burlap bag arced across the firelight and landed upon the ground. It hit with a wet squelch. Agrin, Bijan and the other thugs stared at it in confusion, especially as they noted the bottom of the bag seemed damp and saturated. It was hard to tell in the low light.

"Open it," Abdelkrim said calmly.

Agrin snatched the sack up and clumsily pried the knotted cords open. He looked within and gasped, dropping the bag back to the ground as if having touched a hot iron. The bag bounced and fell open. From its interior rolled something Bijan and the others could not immediately identify. Then, someone cried out once the sickening reality became evident. The head of Abdelkrim's father flopped onto its side, mouth agape and wide eyes unseeing, blood, dripping flesh and pieces of neck bone extant.

"We had a most interesting reunion," Abdelkrim commented from the dark.

"By Allah," whispered Bijan.

Agrin stared at the bloody thing at his feet as small choking noises emerged from his throat. Then he lashed out, kicking the head like a football, sending it sailing back out beyond the fire. "I don't care," he roared. "You think killing a stupid drunkard makes you a man? You, who hid for years out in the desert like a damned jackal? Come out and let us see you again, goosaleh. Come out, if you're not a coward."

"As you wish." A rustle, then into the light stepped a Titan. Abdelkrim had changed. He was naked save for a loincloth of goatskin and a leather belt. A hewn stone knife lay slung in a makeshift sheath at his hip. Abdlekrim's black hair had grown long, flowing wildly down past his shoulders like a curtain of onyx, while his beard was thick and hacked only slightly shorter. Years of exposure to sun and rain and wind had beaten and thickened his skin into a heavy bronze shade. No longer was he the thin, sickly child they had known. The wilderness had hardened him, changed the muscles on arm and leg and chest to rock-hard solidity. The greatest change, however, was his size. Perhaps it was due to his feral lifestyle. Perhaps it was a hidden factor in his genetics. Perhaps he had simply gone through an unusual growth spurt. Regardless, sometime during his hermitage in the mountains, the boy Abdelkrim had become a mountain of a man. He was approaching seven feet in height.

Even the opium-eaters now took note of the new arrival. Slowly, they picked themselves up and cautiously joined their comrades.

"Country life has been good to me," Abdelkrim observed calmly.

Throughout all this, the unfortunate girl Agrin had kidnapped had still been held tightly by Babak. At the first sight of Abdelkrim, however, the astonished thug loosened his grip. Swiftly, the girl twisted out of his grasp and, gasping, threw herself at the giant's feet, casting her arms out imploringly. "Please, sir. Save me from these men. If you call yourself a Muslim, have mercy on me."

It almost seemed to take a moment for Abdelkrim to hear her pleas. He gazed down at her as if truly noticing her presence for the first time. "Mercy?" he asked. "You wish me to show you mercy?"

"Please!"

"Why?"

The question took her aback. "Because–because you are a Muslim!"

"Am I?"

"Are you not? *Please*, sir–"

"Mercy..." Abdelkrim was now looking away from her, chin lifted, staring out into space, mulling the past. "Mercy. Where was mercy when these very men were beating me into the earth where everyone could see, and none would help? Where was mercy when my father whipped me with his belt, leaving my back torn and scarred? I saw no such thing as mercy then. I do not believe it even exists. But" –he looked back at the girl– "I should feed you to my brother here...Pashmir!"

From the shadows a pair of green glowing emeralds suddenly flared. Then the leopard appeared. It, too, had changed much over the ensuing years. It moved with the smooth fluidity of the river, muscles rippling beneath gold and black fur. It silently padded into the firelight, a magnificent expression of feral beauty.

Abdelkrim pointed at the girl. "Are you hungry, my brother?"

The leopard uttered a short growl in reply, licking its lips intently.

Abdelkrim raised an arm, as though ready to command the beast to attack. He paused, stared at the pitiful wreck begging in the dirt before him. Seconds dragged on. Then, he dropped his arm slowly. The leopard remained still by its master's side. "Let it be known this day that I have granted this woman her life. Where no one had shown me mercy, *I* now show it. For the first–and last–time, I give you mercy." He helped the girl up. "Go quickly. For I intend to spill much blood this night. My thirst for it is not yet sated."

The girl said nothing, but slid quickly away into the darkness beyond.

"By Allah," Bijan said in a hoarse whisper.

"Agrin," Abdelkrim turned to face his childhood tormentor. "I came back to this wretched place to exact my revenge. My father was the first to feel my wrath. You all are next."

Agrin stepped forward, arrogant defiance written all over his face. "Who are you to say such things? You are nothing but a gooseleh. Little goosaleh goh. You may have grown large. You may have some trained pet you use to scare people. You don't scare me. You are still the son of a drunken pig and I will send you where pigs belong."

Abdelkrim grit his teeth. He had waited for this moment. Dreamed of it. Now he would take great pleasure in rendering each of them limb from limb.

Agrin grunted and launched himself at Abdelkrim. Agrin was tall and strong. He was also lazy and stupid, arrogant and facile. He took a swing at Abdelkrim, who side-stepped the blow with ease. Agrin swung with another, with the same result. Then another, and another. None landed. "Argghh. Stand still and fight, goosaleh."

The attack continued, with the others all watching on in silence, undoubtedly not knowing what to think or do. Abdelkrim easily dodged and danced his way around every attempted attack Agrin could think of, further enraging the bully.

"Fight. Fight!"

He took another swing, this time at the side of Abdelkrim's head. The latter stopped the blow with a powerful hand, gripping Agrin's tightly, squeezing harder, causing Agrin to wince in pain. Abdelkrim pulled him close...and smiled broadly in his face.

Agrin was stunned. His expression, a mixture of confusion and horror, is one which Abdelkrim will never forget. And one he will savor forever. An instant later, Abdelkrim brought his other arm down powerfully on Agrin's captured arm, breaking it in half with a sickening cracking of bone and tissue. As Agrin screamed in positive agony, dropping to his knees, Abdelkrim, with one swift, powerful motion, took the bully's entire arm off at the shoulder. With blood gushing from the open wound, Abdelkrim tossed the limb aside as so much flotsam. Agrin fell down unconscious in the dirt. He would bleed to death there, Abdelkrim intended. In the dirt, like the animal he was.

"By Allah," Bijan repeated, this time in even more hushed tones than before.

Abdelkrim wasted no more time. He plowed through the rest of the hapless gang in quick time, showing them absolutely no mercy. None were were even remotely capable of defending themselves from a man that had become in that moment a pure killing machine.

In mere moments, the battle, if one could call it that, was over. Bodies, and body parts, lay all around Abdelkrim like garbage strewn on a city street. He was covered in blood. So what? He relished it, realizing he had never felt this alive in his life. Destiny had its man, and he was heeding her call.

A sound to his left broke him from his reverie. "Show yourself," he boomed.

It was merely the girl whom he had shown mercy only a few minutes earlier. She stepped fully into the light.

"Go home," he said to her again.

Others emerged from the shadows, villagers who had been drawn outside by the intense slaughter in their streets.

"Master," the girl said, taking a few more steps toward him. "How may we serve you?"

~ Chapter 5 ~

"And thus, I took my first baby steps toward my destiny," the Cobra mused. "I had taken revenge on my father and my childhood nemesis. I had gained for myself control of my home village. But I was not yet the Cobra. I was still Abdelkrim. A changed man, most certainly. The villagers now did my bidding, even paying homage to me. I made them work. I taught them the meaning of true labor."

Khan made a gurgling sound, but the Cobra went on. He started pacing again. "I had them tend the fields–both vegetable and poppy. Everything was now done in service to me. In time, the fields grew, and I found new, greater markets for our product. The village prospered, and with it, its people. Initially, the followed me out of fear. In time, they came to worship me, as I demanded all others thereafter would."

"Worship my lord," Khan said blankly.

"Did the Iranian authorities know of my little opium ring, Khan? I'm sure they did. They did nothing. Why should they? The Shah ruled, and corruption was the name of the game. Crossing a few palms with silver easily eliminated any potential problems. I learned much those first few years. Learned how to lead men and make them work for me. Learned the basics of finance and the power of money. It was a start. But as I continued to expand my empire, such as it was, I became aware of a great lacking in my life. The lack of education and experience."

"Yes, yes," Khan mumbled.

"Formal education for myself had never been a priority to my village or my father. I had never been to school. Now I began to realize how truly illiterate and uneducated I was— and to realize that, to master the world, that would have to change. I began by acquiring basic textbooks. Teaching myself reading, writing, and simple math. Then more advanced subjects—algebra, chemistry, physics. Late into the night, I would pore over the contents of my books. I found most of it quite easy. Nothing proved too difficult. I already possessed strength and endurance, in time I would have intelligence as well. I began to teach myself other languages. Soon I had mastered no less than seven. Yet I was still not finished. My education, I felt, was complete. Now I needed experience. So, I took the profits from my opium ring...and went to university."

Khan sputtered some gibberish once again.

"Oh, not the campuses of Cambridge or the Sorbonne, you understand, Khan. There would be no stodgy lecture halls for one such as I, no antiseptic laboratories. I already knew all I needed to have to attend those dull places. My university would be quite different. My place of learning would be the back alley and the gambling den; the college of the drug lord and the terrorist. The Triads of Shanghai and Hanoi were my professors. The Yakuza and Mafia my deans. I met bomb-makers in Belfast and Neo-Nazis in Argentina. I gained unofficial diplomas in artillery and gun-running. And everywhere I went, I learned. I made contacts. I grew."

"Nazis...Nazis..."

"Yes, Khan. But I was not yet the Cobra. My destiny was not yet fulfilled. Not until during one trip when I met the professor who would teach me the most. I did not know it at the time. But that mad, cackling half-imbecile was the one that first told me about the mystic power that flows through my veins."

* * * * * *

HAITI - YEARS EARLIER

The road, if it could be called such, was a ground-level cauldron of sucking mud and biting mosquitoes. At each step, Abdelkrim's foot sank four inches into black, stinking mire. He grimaced as he attempted to pull his boot from the muck. It was so stuck he nearly pulled his entire leg out instead.

Haiti was an ugly country. Filthy and unsanitary, even by Iranian standards. The hotel he stayed in was little better than living out on the streets. The human waste that lived there, he felt, were worse than those he dominated back home. Impoverished, ignorant, worthless sheep. He was tired of their stares. He understood the reason—they had rarely seen anyone his sheer size–but the blank non-recognition of his natural superiority in them irked him. They looked at him as if *he* was the freak. These black gnats should be dropping to their knees when he passed by, not simply gawking at him like fish in an aquarium.

In truth, Abdelkrim had never intended to go there in the first place. By this point, his travels around the world, learning all he could, were complete. He had gained all the knowledge he felt necessary, and there was now little more for him to master. By then, he was uncertain of where to go. Abdelkrim knew his destiny was pre-ordained, but as to what it wanted him to do then was anyone's guess. Fate was a capricious thing. It had promised him the world, but so far, it had only made him a glorified drug dealer. It had promised him much more. How was he to find it?

His plan had been to stay in Paris a while, reacquainting himself with Le Milieu before returning to Iran. Yet he had felt a strange...what was it? Not a vision, not like the one he had had. He had felt more...a calling. A peculiar sense that he *should* go to Haiti and see what was there. Why, he did not know. But he felt the call, and so he went.

He soon regretted it. The moment he had arrived, the strange sense of calling had faded, and he rapidly became bored. The criminal and terror elements here were not very interesting or helpful to him. After three days, he decided to leave on the first plane the next morning. But then, that very night, he felt the sensation again. Some odd nagging crawl in his head, on the very edge of consciousness, telling him he needed to go somewhere. Do something. And as Abdelkrim concentrated on it, it seemed to be telling him to travel into the back country of the island. He could just feel it.

Abdelkrim did not believe in any kind of god. But he did believe in Fate, fickle as it could be. So, not knowing exactly where to go, he left Port au Prince, and headed into the countryside, Fate as his guide.

After walking for some days, he found himself in the sparsely-populated section of the Haitian hills, where the people were even more impoverished than their city fellows. Homes there were tarps thrown over strung wire, corrugated metal sheets formed into crude huts, even packing boxes stolen from wherever. He saw few trees. The need for wood for fire and cooking had devastated the ecology of this half of the island. Whereas the Dominican Republic on the other side was filled with greenery, most of Haiti was bare.

Pacing next to him, Pashmir growled and seemed to shudder. Something was clearly disturbing the cat. The fact the great leopard was strolling beside him far from Iran without leash or muzzle was not surprising. Abdelkrim never went anywhere without his brother, sneaking the cat into every country he had visited. Where he felt it safe to do so, they trod their path together.

Abdelkrim reached out and gently stroked the silken fur. "Steady, my brother," he said. "I sense it too. We are being watched."

Rumbling deep in its throat, Pashmir sniffed the air and slunk closer to its master. Abdelkrim frowned. He had never known his brother to be so unnerved. Whatever the cat was sensing was not good.

"Ho, Great Snake!"

Abdelkrim's grip upon Pashmir's scruff grew a little tighter. The leopard arced his back and showed its fangs.

"Ho, Great Snake! Do not be afraid! It is just me, just old, old me! A-heh-heh-heh-heh!"

It was an aged and cracked voice, creaky and trembling. But it rang out loudly enough. Abdelkrim stopped in the middle of the road as, from around the corner about ten yards away, a bent, twisted figure wobbled into view, hobbling along with a long, tweedy stick. He was the most emaciated man Abdelkrim had ever seen. He could count every rib poking through the man's warty, spotty skin. The man was old, perhaps in his eighties, if not older. As he neared, Abdelkrim could see the bald head without even a fringe of hair, the black, toothless gums, the ears that stuck out like birds' wings. The elderly figure did not stop as he saw the giant and cat. He kept right on coming–slowly, painfully, tending a body clearly in pain–but still coming.

Abdelkrim huffed dismissively. *Just an old man who long ago should have tumbled into his grave.* He would have ignored him and moved on past.

The man then croaked out in his crooked voice, "Ho, Great Snake! Mighty General! We who are about to die salute you!"

At that moment a fragment of memory of his vision passed once again across Abdelkrim's eyes. The sight of thousands of men and women, all races and colors, holding up their hands in salute and adoration: "WE HAIL YOU, GREAT ONE! WE WHO ARE ABOUT TO DIE SALUTE YOU!"

Abdelkrim took a step back, momentarily stunned. By now the old man had reached them. Leaning on his makeshift cane, he bowed forward and Abdelkrim could see his eyes. Or rather, he could see the sickly yellow film covering where his eyes should have been. Abdelkrim frowned. Whomever he was, this ancient pile of living sticks was quite blind.

"Heh. A-heh-a-heh-a-heh. Yes, big man, I can't see, I can't see you. I don't know what you look like. But I do know you."

"Know me? You have never met me before, old man."

"No, no, no, never met you before. A-heh-a-heh-a-heh. But I *know* you, Great Snake, *know* you and *what* you are. One

doesn't need eyes to know things, you know. A-heh-heh-heh!
There are other ways of knowing."

Abdelkrim was silent. The old man stood there, grinning
his toothless smile, clearly waiting for the other to say
something. Pashmir growled. The old man merely smiled.
Pashmir bristled and slunk closer to its master.

Abdelkrim felt an unfamiliar sensation of acute
discomfort. For a moment, he considered simply killing the
man and moving on. But if he wanted answers, he would
have to stay his hand.

"As I said, one doesn't need eyes to see everything," the
old man broke into Abdelkrim's thoughts. "Past, future, the
spirit world—all can be seen without eyes if you know how."

Abdelkrim spat. "I do not believe in spirits."

"But you believe in visions. You believe in Fate."

"I...who *are* you?" Abdelkrim bristled.

"A houngan some would call me. Others might call me a
seeker into the spirit realms. Still others, a sorcerer or
warlock. Names, names. They are all the same to me. *I* know
who I am."

A dreadful yet awesome thought was forming in
Abdelkrim's mind. Could it be? "You...knew I was coming
here, didn't you?"

"Knew?" the old man snorted. "I *called* you. Yes, called
you, called you, and you answered. Called you with the
power of my mind! A-heh-heh-heh-heh-heh!"

"Called me..." Abdelkrim frowned. What he was hearing
seemed unbelievable, and yet.... "Let us assume I believe you,
old man. *Why* did you call me here? What do you want of
me?"

"Me? Me? Nothing. I don't want anything of you, Great
Snake—a-heh-heh-heh. It's somebody else who wants you,
wishes to give you what you are seeking."

Abdelkrim stepped forward, as close to the decrepit old figure as he could get. He put his face right up against the veiled eyes. "What somebody else? Who are you speaking of, old man? I demand you tell me."

"Oh, he has many names, many names. Here he is Damballah. Somewhere else he is Yig, somewhere else Set or Apep. Names, names, all the same to him. *He* knows who he is."

"I know these names—at least that of Damballah and Set. Serpent gods. Myths. I do not believe in gods."

"Ah, true, true, but might they not believe in you? A-heh-heh-heh-heh-heh. Doesn't matter what you believe, it matters who you are. And you are one who has been touched by Damballah, Great Snake. Yes, touched. You are his avatar. His first children, the Serpent Men, have failed. Now he chooses you to be his voice."

Abdelkrim stood in stony, incredulous, silence.

"I see you don't believe me," the old man continued. "Well, go ahead, don't believe. Does not matter what you believe, it matters who you arc. But I can see the road you tread. I can see your visions. And I warn you—you have a long way to go yet. You have much to learn. You will make mistakes. And you will fail, unless you capture the power."

"Power? What do you mean by that? I *have* power."

"Power of money, yes. Strength, some. But *power*—the power to truly dominate men? No, you do not have that yet."

"And you do?"

"Me? Oh nonononono. Only power this old man has is to foresee. No other power here. For *your* power, first you must become the Great Snake. You must find the Cult of the Cobra for that. Their time is done, too, mighty Yig has abandoned them. They just don't know it yet. A-heh-heh-heh-heh-heh. But it is where you must begin. Then, you must seek and conquer the Disciple. Conquer him and take what he has for yourself. But be warned—partial conquest will not do. You must conquer *all* of him and take *all* of what he has. Otherwise..."

"What?" Abdelkrim demanded.

"Otherwise the other one shall get it."

His patience at an end, Abdelkrim seized the old man by the worn fabric of his shirt, and lifted him high into the air. Abdelkrim shook him like a baby's rattle. "I grow tired of riddles, fool. Tell me what you are talking about."

"Ah. Ah. All right, all right. Let me down. Ahhh, good to feel good solid earth again, yes? A-heh-heh-heh." But the laugh no longer sounded amused. The old man pulled himself up upon his stick and suddenly it seemed to Abdelkrim the comical figure was not so comical after all, not quite so sickly. Suddenly, the very air about him seemed to darken and become colder, and his voice turned sterner and less cracked. "You tire of riddles, Abdelkrim? Yes, I know your name. Hear me. The laws of the loas decree there must be balance. All things must have its opposite. Black and white. Life and death. Good and evil. Darkness and light. The Great Serpent must strike at a heel, but someone must strike at its head. You shall be opposed. Opposed by one equal to you. He shall trail you, always, always, like an invisible wraith in the night. The battle between life and light, death and darkness, shall be fought between you, again and again, for eons if you allow it. But, eventually, only one can emerge the victor. It might be you. But it might also be he."

Abdelkrim snorted.

"Very soon you will be approached by a man who shall offer you the world, then betray you. Then you shall have a kingdom of your own. If you follow your destiny there, you shall have your power. But if you fail, your opponent will gain that power for himself. In the battle that will follow, you shall walk upon a knife's edge that shall determine the validity of your vision. Either you shall ascend into the heavens—or you shall not. And if you do not, the only way to go is down."

Abdelkrim found himself unconsciously taking another step back, so astonished was he. His mind was awhirl. *An opponent? Threatening me? Threatening my foretold destiny?*

"Yes," the old man said, as if reading the thought. "You shall have an opponent. The only one of two who are your equal. There shall be another as well, of a sort, but that wraith" —he smiled, briefly— "that one shall be quite different from you. But still the same A-heh-heh-heh-heh."

Abdelkrim was now utterly disconcerted, a feeling he did not appreciate in the least. "And just how will I know these two *equals?*" he asked at last.

"You will know them when they remind you of your childhood."

Abdelkrim took a sharp intake of air. Somewhere along the line he had lost control of this situation. It was time to reclaim it. "Now I know you are mad, old man. You may know my vision, but I know my vision does not lie. I cannot fail in my destiny to rule this world. No one can oppose me. Crawl into a corner and die, ancient fool."

"A-heh. A-heh-heh. A-heh-heh-heh-heh-heh-heh-heh-heh!" The old man perked back up, threw his head back and quaked from deep within himself. "So you say, Great Snake. So you say. But the wraith that shall follow you may make you eat those words. But that is tomorrow. Go now and see what comes. Begone. We shall not meet again. A-hehehehehehehehehehehehehehehe!"

And suddenly, the old man lifted his stick and brought it crashing down to the muddy earth. Abdelkrim cried out. Just as the tip of it had struck the ground, a blinding flash of light, as if of a hundred suns, exploded into his eyes. He heard Pashmir yowl and felt him dart away, yelping as it fled. Abdelkrim covered his face with his hands, groaning with the unexpected pain.

But just as suddenly as the flash and pain had come, it vanished. It simply wasn't there anymore. Abdelkrim lifted his face, and opened his eyes. He could see clearly, as if there had never been a flash at all. No after-images. Pashmir, too, stopped and shook its head, as if puzzled as to what was going on. Abdelkrim was puzzled, too. The old man was not there anymore. Like the blindness, he was simply gone. He could not have gone back along the road. He could not have passed Abdelkrim. And there were no trees to hide him on either side.

Abdelkrim had had enough. "Come, Pashmir," he ordered. Instantly, Pashmir was with him, obviously glad to be leaving. Abdelkrim hated to admit it, but so was he.

But as they turned to retrace their steps, Abdelkrim seemed to hear the old man's laughter ringing out behind them. It followed them all the way back to Port-au-Prince.

* * * * * *

"Who was he, Khan? I do not know. Perhaps...I do not want to know. But he was right. In every way, he was right. I think that frightened me–frightens me still–most of all."

~ Chapter 6 ~

PARIS - YEARS EARLIER

"Pardonnez-moi, m'sieu, mais series-vou M'sieu... Abdelkrim?"

The unexpected question brought Abdelkrim out of his black reverie. With some annoyance, he noted that a very excellent basil salmon terrine had only been picked at, and the main course, a platter of duck l'orange, was cold. The volumes he had just purchased from a local bookstore remained unread.

It was one of the finest early spring afternoons Paris had seen in quite some time. The temperature was warm yet dry, with a cooling breeze starting to float gently off the Seine. A Sunday, there was little traffic on the roads, but young couples and families strolled up and down the paths in Champ de Mars, laughing gaily and tasting ice cream. Gray pigeons flapped and fluttered, cooing and strutting alongside the benches where elderly men tossed them peanuts and bread crumbs. Unusually, there were few tourists wandering about. Those that were gawked stupidly while snapping photos of the Eiffel Tower and speaking bad French. It was too splendid a day to pay them much attention, even to someone as important as Abdelkrim.

It had been three weeks since he had left Haiti, and he was still haunted by his strange encounter. The sudden disappearance of the old man no longer unnerved him as much. He rationalized that as some sort of trick, having watched stage magicians do much the same thing, knowing all the while it was simply an illusion. The old man had *not* vanished into thin air. Could not have. There was no such thing as magic, he felt certain of that.

But there might yet be such a thing as mysticism. There might yet be lost and hidden powers at work in this world. Abdelkrim did acknowledge that possibility. His visions had been mystic, and the old man had somehow known of them. The same power that had touched Abdelkrim had, somehow, touched him too. That was the only explanation that made any sense to him. But the old man's words haunted him even more.

You shall be opposed. Look to the Cult of the Cobra. Seek and conquer the Disciple. Take all *his power. You shall be opposed.... You will know them when they remind you of your childhood.*

What could all that possibly mean?

At least Pashmir had seemed to recover fully. Once away from Haiti he had calmed considerably.

"Do you know who I am?"

The query was still in French, but Abdelkrim knew that accent. Iranian. A fellow countryman. Abdelkrim wanted no

SERPENT RISING | **61**

company but his own thoughts that day. He was about to reply coldly, when he realized he *did* know whom his addresser was. Like the Haitian, he was old, though still, strictly speaking, much younger in age. He was dressed in the severe, simple robes of a Muslim cleric: black qabaa, inexpensive but comfortable slippers, a turban the same shade as his robe. A long grizzled beard, salt and pepper slowly turning to pure white, hung from his chin. On the surface, just another old mullah. But it was his eyes that were the most arresting thing about him. They were intense gems, glittering out at the world with a zealous fanaticism that hypnotized. Oh yes, Abdelkrim knew this man. Everyone in the Shah's Iran did.

"I am Ruhollah Khomeini. Ayatollah of the Faith. I have heard much about you. M'seiu Abdelkrim." Without being invited, he slipped into the chair across from Abdelkrim.

Slowly, a long, grim smile began to cross Abdelkrim's face. He reached for the bottle of wine upon the table and poured himself a fresh glass. "Indeed. And I have heard of you, Ayatollah. Few people from Iran have not."

Khomeini watched the red liquid flow disapprovingly. "The Prophet, peace be upon him, has forbidden the drinking of alcohol to those of the True Faith."

"Hmph. So I have heard." Abdelkrim raised the glass to his lips and sipped placidly. "Fortunately, I do not claim to be a follower of the True Faith. So, I may drink whatever I so desire."

Khomeini began to rise, words of protest upon his lips.

Abdelkrim briefly chuckled, then frowned at the man opposite. "Sit down," he snarled. "You intrigue me. Your confidence and...fire...amuses me."

Khomeini sat.

"Now, tell me what you want of me. I know well the Shah exiled you and your family from Iran. I presume this little visit concerns an attempt for you to return."

"The Shah!" The Ayatollah spat upon the ground. "That westernized pig. Pretender to Islam and servant to Jews. We must sweep him and his ilk aside and return our country to the proper tenants of the Faith. I *shall* sweep him aside."

Abdelkrim watched this little spasm with some amusement. "I note the Shah has not been in good health recently."

"No. Allah in His wisdom has finally decided to punish him. Cancer. Doctors are treating him, but it has grown so bad the Shah has all but withdrawn from public life. This is a good thing. Our countrymen are discontent to say the least, Abdelkrim. They tire of Pahlavi's western ideas, his relationship with the damned Israelis, and the corruption of his government. A breath of wind, and his dictatorship shall fall."

Abdelkrim took another sip. "And? What has that to do with me?"

"I know who you are, my friend. I know the extent of the...organization you lead."

"*And?*" Abdelkrim grew tired of the conversation.

"You are no friend of the Shah."

Abdelkrim stared into the glass and swished the dregs of his wine around slowly. "No. Nor am I his enemy, per sé."

The older man leaned forward eagerly. "Join with me, Abdelkrim. I am the most powerful cleric in Iran. I command the discontented faithful. You are its most powerful...secular person. You have influence where I do not. Help me cause enough discontent to overthrow the Shah. *Now* is the time to strike. Together we can take over Iran and–and–"

SERPENT RISING | 63

"Return it to the True Faith?" Abdelkrim smirked. "I know you as well, M. Khomeini. You are a zealot. You would put our homeland as thoroughly beneath your heel as the Shah does." *As I will, too, once the world is mine.*

"I need you. I need your organization."

"And what would I get in return?"

The Ayatollah sighed. "In return, I would be willing...to overlook your atheism. You would gain control not just some of Iran's underworld, but all of it. I am no fool. The criminal underclass shall not vanish just because I bring Iran back to the Faith. It shall simply go deeper underground. It shall be yours. In exchange for your help when I need it."

"Doing what, precisely?" Abdelkrim's interest grew, faintly.

"I do not intend to cease with just Iran. The west must pay for its apostasy. The Great Satan has interfered in our internal affairs too long. I require—*experts*—who know how to cause turmoil and strife. In our country and theirs. I believe you can fulfill that need, M. Abdelkrim."

"I see." Abdelkrim leaned back in his chair. As much as he craved power—resolute, sole dominion over all—he knew he was not yet ready. Perhaps the Ayatollah's suggestion was a good first step? "Well. This is an interesting proposition."

"I can give you the world, M. Abdelkrim," the Ayatollah promised.

"The world?" *I shall give myself the world.* "We shall see. But. Come to my suite tonight, Ayatollah. I am staying in the Palais Iena. We shall speak more. Good day to you."

Abdelkrim tossed some bills upon the table, rose, and turned his back upon his guest, strolling casually away. He knew Khomeini was watching him go. He also knew the thoughts going through the elder man's head. He knew the Ayatollah would use him, and the power he already yielded, but would betray him as soon as was feasible. The Ayatollah would never accept to share power over Iran for long. Abdelkrim smiled as he walked. *But I shall use you too, old man. You shall be my tool in gaining power for myself. Eventually we shall clash. But that day is not today. For now —I shall play the apprentice. But soon I shall become the Master.*

* * * * * *

"And lo, my first true deal with the devil, Khan," the Cobra said, pacing before his lackey. "I found it convenient. History will tell you what came next. The Shah grew more ill. The young and disaffected–thanks to the Ayatollah's pressure and my own subtler efforts–became more and more incensed. Finally, upon Black Friday, the insurrection occurred. The Shah fled into exile. Iran wished him back for trial. But he became more ill and, ever the self-righteous humanitarians, America agreed to accept him for treatment."

"M...master," Khan sputtered.

"The time was soon at hand for my next move," the Cobra said, ignoring his servant. "On February 1, 1979 the Ayatollah Khomeini returned in triumph to Iran from his exile in France. The people exalted. I had been back long before. No one had noticed. But I had been moving, planning behind the scenes. Khomeini and his fanatics were content with turning Iran into a Shiite paradise. I intended to turn it into my personal fiefdom. But if I failed, I had put events in motion even the Ayatollah did not expect. But those plans were not yet ready to be put into motion. Fate, as always, had its own plans for me. I could not know that, as I toiled toward my destiny in Iran, in another country, things were being set for my future. The old man's words would yet come to pass."

* * * * * *

MOSCOW - YEARS EARLIER

There could not have been a more faceless man in all the Soviet Union. He was as plain and ordinary and unremarkable as possible. There was no point in trying to describe him for there was nothing to describe. You could see him every day and forget him as soon as you had seen him. There was absolutely nothing of note about him. Clad in a tattered raincoat against the foul weather, carrying a battered attaché case, there was nothing to do but ignore him. It was an image calculated precisely for that reason.

The rain pelted down. The faceless man stepped along, past people in wet queues hoping the bread and milk might still be available at the store when they arrived. Past soaked clerks rushing back to their small bureaucratic offices, past mechanics sneaking out of their garages for a quick smoke and past unknown people going unknown places but making sure they were all going somewhere. It did not pay to be idle in the Worker's Paradise. He passed others as well, as equally faceless and unnoticeable as he. These he recognized as members of the Secret Police. If they noticed him, he did not worry. A quick flash of his identification would result in his swift release from any questioning. And an equally swift trip to Siberia for the overzealous agent.

The faceless man left the busy street behind and soon entered a residential area. A narrow street made up on both sides of small, soot-encrusted apartments crushed together like brick accordions. His previous slow, shuffling gait had ceased. He now walked like a man knowing precisely where he was going. His fingers tightened upon the attaché's handle as he mounted a set of cracked steps to one door and boldly rang the bell.

From the other side he could hear steps approaching. Then the soft metallic click of a peephole flipped open. There was a long pause. The faceless man raised an eyebrow expectantly. The click again–the peephole closed–and the faceless man fancied he heard a sigh on the other side of the door. Then it slowly opened. It was not often the faceless man caught his breath. But the vision that greeted him framed in the dull gray light always did. She was a portrait come to life, Galatea given flesh. Her face should have graced the cover of a Paris magazine, not the threshold of a drab Soviet flat.

"Comrade," she greeted softly.

Her figure was flawless. Clad as it was in a simple house dress, fit to wear only for cleaning and cooking, her fine, high bosom and athletic curves still shone forth. The tall willowy slenderness of her frame only accentuated the faceless man's inconspicuous size. Her skin was flawless porcelain, the long hair black as purest onyx. Deep violet eyes completed the ensemble of absolute feminine perfection. But the beauty of those eyes could not hide their concern and fear as the statuesque beauty regarded the plain man standing silently before her.

"Comrade," she repeated. "Please..."

The faceless man shook his head. "No. He is needed."

"For...for how long this time?" The query was a hoarse whisper.

The faceless man's own voice was stonily impassive. "For a while. Possibly a long while."

"*Please*–"

"No."

"Who is it, Elisabet?" The voice spoke out from further in the house. "Who is at the do–oh. Greetings, Comrade."

The faceless man nodded. "Blackov."

The face that peered over the woman's shoulder was as handsome as hers was beautiful, the close-cropped hair as dark as his wife's. His own eyes were emerald green to her violet, and his skin was bronzed from the toil of foreign suns. He was ruggedly built, but moved with the same masterful poise as the woman next to him, who had graced the Moscow ballet with her beauty and talent. It seemed almost unworldly to see two such physically perfect specimens in such drab surroundings.

The faceless man indicated his case. "May I come in?"

"Of course. Elisabet, my love, tea for our guest, if you please."

Elisbet Blackova looked at her husband with distressed eyes. "Piotr..."

Piotr gently put a finger to her lips. "Hush. Fetch the tea."

Elisabet retreated to the kitchen, but the fact she was not pleased was obvious to both men. Piotr gestured his guest inside. "Come in, Comrade. Let me get your coat. Wretched weather, eh?"

"Da. Typical Moscow autumn."

"Come into the living room." Piotr led the way down the small, sparsely-furnished hall.

Midway across, a stairway intersected, leading up to a second story. The faceless man glanced upwards. At the top of the stairs, clutching a raggedy doll in her arms, stood a tiny girl of about four or five. Piotr smiled at the sight. "Natalya," he said warmly. Leaving his comrade, he took the stairs two at a time to snatch her up in his arms.

The faceless man watched Natalya Blackova press her face against her father's shoulder. She was a child, but she possessed her mother's eyes and hair and was already showing signs of her gracefulness. "Papa, it's that man again. I don't like him. Every time he comes you have to go away."

Piotr cupped his hand beneath her chin, forcing her to meet his eyes. "He is my employer, Natalya. I must do as he says. Now go back to your room like a good girl. I cannot be interrupted."

"Will you come and play tea with me later?"

"I will try, my love. It depends on what our comrade has for me to do. Go on, now." Gently he pushed her off.

"You have a beautiful family, my friend," the faceless man said as Piotr returned.

"Thank you. I love them very much."

"As much as you love the Party?"

Piotr met his gaze evenly. "No. The needs of the People always come first."

"Excellent. Then let us speak."

* * * * * *

Eisabet sat the tray of tea and scones upon the table and glared at her husband.

"Thank you, my dear," Piotr told her. "Now, please, leave us. Our Comrade and I have much to discuss." Elisabet left the room in silence. Piotr sipped from his cup and took a bite of scone. "So...what is happening in the world?"

The faceless man pushed the tray aside and placed his attaché case upon the table. He opened it and removed a manila file, tossing it to his companion. "You are aware of what is happening in Iran?"

Piotr opened the file and started scanning its contents. "Of course. Who is not?"

"Then you know of our interests in the region."

"I do."

"Have you heard the name Abdelkrim?"

Piotr frowned. "Some kind of legendary Muslim warrior, I believe. Morocco?"

"No. This one operates today, in Iran. I–we–have a great interest in this man."

Piotr turned a page. "Is this he? A monster of a man."

"Our best artist's interpretation. There is no known photograph of the man. But he has been on our radar for some time. He started out as an opium grower in Iran. Within the last several years, however, he has begun branching out."

"A Muslim zealot, of course."

"Curiously, no, we do not believe so," the faceless man said. "The man seems to have no religious beliefs at all. Yet we know that he has been amassing followers from across Iran and other countries–seemingly just from the force of his own personality. It is still rough, but from what we have put together, it would seem this man is intent on creating his own cult of some kind, or empire. Although what that might entail remains to be seen."

"And what has this to do with me?" Piotr asked, curious but noncommittal.

"Recently, he met with the Ayatollah Khomeini in Paris. I correct myself–the Ayatollah met with *him*. They seem to have struck some kind of bargain. Much of the current unrest in Iran comes not from Khomeini, but from this...Abdelkrim. We know what Khomeini is up to. He is no friend of our Worker's Utopia any more than he is of the decadent west. But this man, Abdelkrim–he is an unknown factor. He is working *with* Khomeini, but not *for* him. And two such disparate personalities cannot help but clash sooner than later. The People wish to know what this man is up to. Further strife in the region cannot be tolerated. This is where you come in."

"I see. What am I to do?"

The faceless man sipped a bit of tea, made a face and added more sugar. "You are to infiltrate, if you can, this man's organization. You shall find out all you can of his intentions and alert us to them. You shall stay with him as long as you can. If he plots against the People, you shall tell us, and we shall take steps to curtail him. If he plots against the Americans, we shall do what we can to assist him. And if it comes to pass that we deem it necessary...you shall kill him."

"A moment, Comrade. This shall undoubtedly take some time," Piotr said grimly.

The faceless man nodded, utterly impassively. "It may."

"We are not speaking of a matter of weeks or months. We speak of years."

"We do."

"When would I leave?" Piotr said in a determined tone.

"Tomorrow. We have set up an identity for you as a deserter from the Soviet Army. We know Abdelkrim recruits former soldiers when he can."

Piotr put his cup down and took a long breath. "Then I must request something, Comrade. In all this time, I have never asked the People for anything. But today, I have no choice."

* * * * * *

The faceless man stepped out of the house, once more pulling his collar up against the weather. The task for the day had been completed.

He knew the chances of Blackov returning from his mission were slim. He did not care. Piotr was a servant of the People, his life was irrelevant compared to the whole. The faceless man had agreed to Piotr's condition, which was absurdly simple, and that was that.

He should be on his way. But before he left, something made him pause and glance up toward the second story of the building. There, peering out a dirty window, the tiny face of Natalya stared back down at him with a frown. The faceless man managed a wan smile, then he turned and left.

* * * * * *

Natalya Blackova pressed her dolly a little closer. She really did not like the faceless man. She knew he was a bad man who did not like her Papa, no matter how he acted. Already, she knew her Papa would be leaving again. He always did when the faceless man came. And as she watched the nondescript figure walk out into the rain, she swore to herself one thing: if her beloved Papa ever came to harm because of the faceless man, she would kill him herself.

~ Chapter 7 ~

IRAN - YEARS EARLIER

The man with the blindfold moaned softly in his seat. His hands were tied behind his back and his legs roped firmly to the chair's legs. He had long ago stopped shouting his outrage, exhaustion having taken over. By this stage, after three hundred and twenty-one days of being held hostage, it must have been clear his captors were not going to let him go lightly, if at all.

Abdelkrim had no idea who the American was. Some minor clerk, he believed. Not that it mattered, to him or the others who had seized control of the Embassy on November 4 of the previous year. All that mattered was the gnat was an American, which made him an enemy. To the Ayatollah, that was. To Abdelkrim, *everyone* was *his* potential enemy.

"We should kill them all," the young Iranian next to him muttered. "Kill them, and teach the Great Satan that Allah is greater than their infidel country."

"That time may yet come," Abdelkrim murmured. "But not now. The longer we let them live, the longer the Americans shall hope for their release. And the longer we have them under our thumb. To kill them would remove our hold and fear over them. Be patient, and let time take its course."

"If you say so, sir," the youngster replied doubtfully. Like most of the other terrorists, once he had simply been another university student who looked askance at the lack of jobs and other opportunities for him in this corrupt country. He had been perfect fodder for Abdelkrim's cause. The titan couldn't remember his name, but that fact didn't matter to him much. This one was just another of Khomeini's religious fanatics, a warm body to be used and disposed of when finished with. Not someone with whom Abdelkrim would give another thought to.

"Very good," Abdelkrim said dismissively and turned to go. He had only come to the Embassy to check on matters. Everything seemed to be ticking along very smoothly. "Come, Pashmir." Obediently, the leopard trotted after him.

As the two entered the lobby, Abdelkrim paused just long enough to cock an eye at the grand clock upon the wall. He took special note of the exact time. Yes. Things *were* ticking along quite nicely. Matters should be coming to a head very shortly.

His private car, as always, was waiting for him. He nodded briefly to Hijan, his driver, and a new lackey, Mikail Dragovich. Dragovich was a recent Russian deserter, looking to make his mark as a mercenary. Remarkably handsome for a mere soldier, but Abdelkrim had been impressed by his record. Combat in Afghanistan, raids in Poland and Yugoslavia. He had hired the man at once. Abdelkrim slipped into the back, Pashmir crawling in alongside. Bijan and Dragovich climbed into the front and in moments they were moving down the streets of the city.

"Sir," Dragovich said, "You have had a message."

"From whom?"

"The Ayatollah, sir."

Abdelkrim smiled, but feigned ignorance. "I thought he was in Qom."

"No, he is in Tehran. He wishes to meet with you," Dragovich said.

Abdelkrim chuckled and stroked Pashmir. "Then let us not keep him waiting."

* * * * * *

"Abdelkrim."

"Khomeini."

The religious leader rose from his desk, a look of annoyance upon his face. "That is *Ayatollah* Khomeini."

"Khomeini," Abdelkrim replied calmly.

The elderly mullah growled, but retook his chair. "The beast waits outside," he snapped, pointing at Pashmir.

"My brother stays with me," came the answer.

"Outside!"

"No," Abdelkrim said calmly but firmly.

Sensing the tension in the air, Pashmir's back began to arch. A touch of a finger, and the arch subsided. But the fur remained bristled.

"What can I do for you, *Ayatollah?*" Abdelkrim questioned. "I was engaged in other matters when you so rudely summoned me. May I take it you have finally had your fill of me?"

"As always, your prescience is exceeded only by your arrogance," the Ayatollah said harshly. "You speak correctly. It is time for this partnership of ours to be ended. You were useful for a time, but now your usefulness had ended. There is no place for the likes of you and yours in my new Iran. From henceforth, you are to consider yourself an exile from this land. You have precisely twenty-four hours to gather your things, and—"

"A moment, if you please," Abdelkrim held a hand up in defiance. "*You* exile *me?* May I remind you that it was not you but *I* who created this New Iran you speak of? It was *my* plans, *my* genius. Not yours."

"Pah!" Khomeini pounded upon his desk. "*You?* You were a mere tool in the hand of Allah. It was *His* will that drove the Shah out and bid me return to guide this land back into the fold of the True Faith. It was *He* who chose me to return in triumph and cause the Great Satan to shake in his boots. You are His tool, but I am His mouthpiece!"

Abdelkrim laughed. "You believe so? I do not. I did not see Allah stretch forth a divine hand to give us the plans on how best to invade and seize the American embassy. That came from me. You laughed at it, as I recall. Said that it was impossible, that the Americans would shoot anyone who dared raid their compound. Yet, not one American fired a shot. I knew they would not. Americans are cowards at heart. They fear their reputation if they kill innocents and protesters. We took the Embassy. *I* took the Embassy.

"Pah!" the Ayatollah said again.

"And when the American President arranged his little rescue attempt? Did your Allah send lightning from the sky to strike those helicopters down? He did not. I sabotaged them through my agents, having known they were planning it from the start. Oh, Carter came up with a cover tale, naturally. Politicians are so good at covering up their ineptitude. Regardless, at this moment the remains of his attempt lie rusting in the desert thanks to me. Not thanks to any non-existent god!"

The Ayatollah practically leapt from his seat. "BLASPHEMY!" he roared. "Never have I heard such blasphemy, even from the lips of the damnable Jews! I shall have you executed for this outrage. Guards! Ack–"

The elderly man's screams were cut off as Abdelkrim's huge hand suddenly cupped the Ayatollah's throat. "I would not, my friend. I simply would not. Pashmir has not been fed today, and I can hear his stomach rumbling. Be silent, and listen." Abdelkrim tossed Khomeini back into his seat as a child would a rag doll. "Your declarations mean nothing to me. *You* mean nothing to me. I took your initial power sharing offer because I wished to see if I could use you to gain this land for myself. But of late, I see that I am still not ready. True power is not yet mine. There is another land for me, where–if I am correct–a greater destiny awaits me than you could ever grant me. You once told me you could give me the world. I shall *take* the world for myself."

The Ayatollah growled but said nothing.

"I leave Iran, but not because of you. I have other plans. Yet, I have no wish to spend most of my time avoiding your secret murder squads. They are also as nothing to me, but naught must delay me from my destiny. So, I have made certain arrangements."

Khomeini rubbed his throat, trying to get his breath back. "Whu–what do you mean?"

Abdelkrim smiled. "It is no secret you have been itching to spread your version of Islam to the neighboring countries, particularly Iraq. After all, both lands were once one until the English broke Persia in two. You and Saddam Hussein have no love for each other. You've been planning an invasion for some time. I have seen the plans. Brilliant, Khomeini. So brilliant, in fact, I gave them to the Iraqis."

"You—what?"

"I gave them to Hussein. He was most happy to receive them. Indeed, he liked them so much he is putting them into play himself—just in the opposite direction. Iraq is going to invade Iran, Khomeini. And you can do nothing to stop it."

Khomeini's eyes were baseballs in their sockets. "When—when is this happening?"

"Oh," Abdelkrim glanced at the clock, "about twenty minutes ago."

The Ayatollah Khomeini screamed. He shot forward, howling curses. Abdelkrim simply swatted him away. "Enough, old fool. I'm leaving now. Undoubtedly you shall issue your death order, but I am not concerned. I suspect you and your people will be a little busy to carry it out. When next you hear from me, it shall be as lord of my own country. Then, I shall be lord of yours." He whipped around and left the office, leaving Khomeini and his screaming invective behind.

Dragovich opened the door to the car when he returned. "Where to next, sir?"

Abdelkrim chuckled. "Eritrea," he said.

* * * * * *

"Why Eritrea, Khan? Why an African land, impoverished, tiny and resource-poor; a mish-mashed agglomeration of former kingdoms possessing little glory or power in the world? Why a country hardly anyone, east or west, knew even existed?"

"Wh...why, Master?" Khan said weakly.

"The old man from Haiti," the Cobra replied. "He guided me there. Ever since our encounter, I had been doing research. Research on serpent cults around the world. The old man had said the Cult of the Cobra would be involved in the next step toward my destiny. After much investigation, I found what I thought I sought. There was an obscure cult that haunted Africa, so obscure very few outside the continent were even aware of it. Those who dwelt in the major cities thought it was but legend, but those that lived in the small villages and kraals, the poor and the ignored, knew it to be quite real. A cult that worshiped so-called Serpent Men that supposedly ruled Earth then fell out of favor long before the rise of humanity."

"Ba...ba..." Khan spouted gibberish.

"I doubted such creatures as Serpent Men actually existed," the Cobra continued. "But the fact someone else believed in them was what mattered. I determined the heart of the cult existed in Eritrea. Therefore, I needed to go and see what awaited me there. There was another point, as well. The old man had spoken of another entity, the Disciple of the Mountains. The person I must steal some kind of power from. I searched everywhere for what he had meant. I pondered over ancient tomes with blasphemous names that told of things that might frighten anyone else with its supposed secrets. And at last, in an ancient Ethiopian manuscript, I found mention of that title. A brief statement of some kind of Holy Man living high in the peaks surrounding Emba Soira that knew of some great secret, of an ancient power forgotten by man. Or some such nonsense.

"Power master," Khan uttered.

"Yes, Khan. I was intrigued. I had to know. If the old man's words were true, this was the key to my destiny. So I resolved to make Eritrea my very own kingdom–even if I had to be the power behind the power. But I did not want to simply arrive there. I wanted my conquest to mean something. So I walked. I gathered my followers–now numbering into the dozens–and walked from Iran to Eritrea on foot, gathering more en route."

"Foot master," Khan said, appearing to become more agitated.

"I shall spare you the telling of my adventures along the way," the Cobra said. "Suffice to say, among other things, the Ayatollah did issue his fatwa, and there were those who attempted to fulfill it. I defeated them all. There were other matters, too, along the way, but they were inconsequential. In time I reached Eritrea alive and well. My idea was to travel to the capital, Asmara, spend some time there, learning the lay of the land and its people then, ultimately, launching a coup. Once that had been accomplished, I would then locate members of the Cobra Cult and bend them to my service. As it turned out, I did not have to come to them at all." The Cobra smiled as the memories flowed. "They came to me."

* * * * * *

ERITREA - YEARS EARLIER

The shallow river wound its way across a barren savanna, turning the muddy banks into a ribbon of green in a brown world. Water birds gently waded across looking for small fish and frogs, and a turtle rested sunning itself on a fallen log. A few palm trees fanned out along the bank, fronds waving in the breeze. In a land of poverty and strife, this was a scene of tropical tranquility. Naturally, it could not last.

They came marching in military-like precision, ramrod straight and clad in army fatigues, although not one of them belonged to the military of any country. There were now only ten or so left. Each carried an air of intense discipline and fierce loyalty. Months ago they had walked out of Iran almost two hundred strong, following in the heels of one man. These were those who had survived the journey. Over mountain and desert they had marched, without the use of plane or vehicle–only their feet. They had faced brutal heat, frigid cold, and the continual assault of man. One by one, the weak had fallen. They had been left behind where they lay. Their master had no use for those not strong enough to survive.

One called Hijan had dropped early in the march. As an opium addict, that had been no surprise. He had served his master as well as he could, but no sympathy had been spared for him. One who had survived was a rugged, remarkably handsome Russian named Mikhail Dragovich. Like the rest he marched in silence, face impassive, but if one looked hard enough, perhaps–just perhaps–they could see a glint of something in Dragovich's eyes. A hint of hatred and disdain. There might have been something else in those eyes, as well, Abdelkrim thought. A wistfulness, as if Dragovich was thinking about something or someone far, far away. Then again, it could simply be imagination.

Before them all marched a giant, a human titan of massive proportions. Though clad in fatigues like the others, Abdelkrim wore them with an effortless air of command. At his side, as always, Pashmir padded, silent and dutiful. The giant never spoke or gazed back at his men, only the briefest brush of a finger across his leopard's back was his only unnecessary motion. His thoughts were heavy that day. They should, if all went well, reach Asmara that night. The capital of Eritrea, Abdelkrim was looking forward to getting there. Although he would never admit it, he was weary of their long journey. Tired of sleeping in sun and rain, on hard ground or muddy. He longed to feel the long-awaited coldness of a crown placed upon his head, to sleep between silk sheets, to finally claim the life of luxury and splendor he deserved. Tonight he would finally find that life.

Or...perhaps not. Perhaps Fate would play him another hand.

His intent, when he had started his long trek, was to seize power in this small land for all the world to see. To declare to one and all the majesty of his being and tell them that, soon, they would be joining the Eritreans under his jackboot. Eritrea would merely be the beginning–a tiny beginning–of what would one day be the greatest empire the world had ever seen. *His* empire! He yearned for it with all his being. And yet–somewhere deep within him, day in and day out, on the very edge of his consciousness, there was a nagging whisper. A still, almost silent voice, much like that of the old man of Haiti, saying softly. "No, not yet. You are not ready yet. Take your rule, but do not advertise it. Be patient. Your day shall come."

It was frustrating, it was irksome. It was intolerable. Yet it was there, and it was insistent. The Cobra grimaced as he considered the idea. *What is the best thing to d–*

So intent was he upon his musings, when he next extended a finger to brush his brother, the digit met nothing but empty air. Abdelkrim looked down, Pashmir was no longer by his side. He looked back. The big cat was yards behind the rest of the group, sitting on his haunches, panting rapidly.

Abdelkrim turned, pushed through his men, and came to his only friend. He knelt down. Not for the first time Abdelkrim noted the graying muzzle, the watery eyes, the loosening teeth. The giant's gaze softened. He reached out a hand and stroked the cat's head. "You grow old, my brother," he said gently. "Old and tired." Abdelkrim was right. The average life-span of a leopard was seventeen years at best. Through Abdelkrim's constant care, Pashmir was now almost twice that. By the standards of his species, Pashmir was not just old, he was ancient. Abdelkrim rose and addressed his men. "We make camp here." Asmara could wait for one more night. There was one thing, and one thing alone, Abdelkrim cared for as much as he did his destiny.

Pashmir had fallen asleep the moment camp was pitched. Abdelkrim set his tent next to where he lay. Now sitting before the fire, the titan watched wistfully as his brother dozed. The night was cold. Abdelkrim used no blanket himself, but tossed one over the leopard to warm him. Pashmir pawed in its sleep and the giant was certain he heard the cat purr. He smiled.

"Sir." In the shadows of the firelight, the figure of Mikhail Dragovich arose. "We have a problem."

"What?"

"I sent Ebrahim and Farzad out on watch two hours ago. For the past half-hour, they have not reported in."

Abdelkrim's eyes narrowed. "You went to find them?"

"Yes, sir. I could not locate them. But I found—"

"Found what, Dragovich?"

"I found blood, sir. A lot of blood."

Abdelkrim leapt to his feet. "Wake the men. Prepare your weapons. We are under attack."

Dragovich raced to obey. Within seconds, the men were scrambling from their tents. Too late. With whoops of wild savagery they broke out of the darkness, dozens of them. They came from all sides, a circle around the camp, blocking all exits. "Seize them!" Abdelkrim heard one yell, an aged voice in broken Swahili.

"Fire!" cried Abdelkrim. Instantly the night air sang out with the explosive *ratatatatat* of automatic weapons. The firelight was too dim to see everything, but from the shadows came screams of agony, and Abdelkrim saw men fall in the distance. "Keep firing!" he ordered, unleashing his own weapon upon the enemy.

Abdelkrim's men had proven their stamina. They had dealt with the worst of conditions and lived to tell of it. But they were still just ten or so men, and it was quickly evident that the attackers outnumbered them, perhaps three to one. For every enemy that went down, two others took their place. Within moments, they had spilled over into the camp. Hand-to-hand combat ensued. The silver of knives flashed in the low light. The sound of noses crunching and bones breaking echoed around them. Abdelkrim seized one attacker, lifted him over his head, and tossed him into four others as though he was made of rags.

For the first time he got a good look at his enemies. Native Africans, as he expected, but not merely a band of thieves roaming the Savannah as he had thought. All of them wore full-body robes that glinted strangely in the dim light. Abdelkrim soon realized the garments were made of snake-skin. With a sudden thrill, it came to him—these were the very members of the Cobra Cult he had come to find.

"Die!"

Abdelkrim whipped around just in time. Mere inches away a cultist was pointing a rifle aimed directly at his heart. There was no time to avoid the blast. The cultist's finger pulled on the trigger–

RRRRRROWWWRRR!!!

A flash of gold and black whizzed by Abdelkrim. He knew instantly what it was. "Pashmir, NO!!"

It was too late. Woken by the commotion, it had seen an enemy threaten the life of its beloved brother. Summoning all the strength it had, Pashmir had rushed forth to his defense. The leopard fell upon the cultist with the speed of a rocket, sprawling with him to earth. Fangs bared, claws tore. A fountain of blood spurted from vulnerable human flesh. But the cultist still had his rifle. Even in his dying moments he aimed blindly and pulled the trigger. Even above the riot, the noise of the blast was deafening. As was the yowl of pain as Pashmir went flying backward.

"NO!" Abdelkrim screamed. "NONONONONO!" Ignoring the cultists, ignoring his men, ignoring everything, he scrambled to his brother's aid. Pashmir was lying upon its side. Abdelkrim saw the gaping hole in there, saw the sickening mix of blood and bone. For the last time, a pair of emerald eyes looked into his. From somewhere deep in its ruined chest, the ancient leopard purred one final time as its human brother gave its coat one final stroke. Then the emerald faded into nothingness.

Abdelkrim stood, feeling a rage in his heart greater than any other he had felt before. "Damn you," he whispered. Then he screamed it. "DAMN YOU! DAMN YOU DAMN YOU DAMN YOU FOR KILING MY BROTHER! YOU SHALL PAY! YOU SHALL ALL PAY!!"

Abdelkrim launched into the attack. He did not count the number of cultists he slew that night. But before it was all over, the Cult of the Cobra knew what vengeance truly was. But even the greatest warrior must fall before superior numbers and fatigue. As the sun slowly began its rise, the fight finally ended. Abdelkrim had gone down, pulled to the ground by a massive piling of men. With some difficulty, they yanked him to his feet, pinned his arms behind his back.

Abdelkrim was now able to see he had lost all his men save one–Mikhail Dragovich, the Russian, remained. He, too, had been taken at the last, though not before scoring his own set of kills. Together the men were hustled away from the camp. It took six men each to drag them along. Both were drenched in blood from the night's battle and each had their own wounds to contend with. But both refused to drop from exhaustion or loss of blood.

Abdelkrim looked back only once. Not toward the slain bodies of his men or his enemies, but at a sprawled body of a great cat. He knew well the ways of the African Savannah. Within hours the predators would come to rip apart the bodies for their daily meal. Then the scavengers. Finally the insects would reduce the meat to bones, and the bones to dust. Within days, there would be little sign that a magnificent beast named Pashmir had ever existed. The realization of this hardened Abdelkrim's soul. He parted his lips. He did not wish his captors to hear, so he whispered. "Goodbye, my brother. I swear to you that you shall be the last being to ever enter my heart. From this day on, I shall carry on alone. I swear to you. Goodbye."

After a march that took quite some time, they arrived at a small village. Abdelkrim and Dragovich were placed separately in cages made of timber. They were cramped even for Dragovich, a large man in his own right. But to one with such a massive frame as Abdelkrim, it was like being thrust inside a broom closet that could fit only one broom. The cultists ensured their prisoners were secured inside, then left them alone with their thoughts.

"Why didn't they kill us?" Dragovich queried after some little time.

Abdelkrim shrugged. "To sell us into slavery, perhaps. Or sacrifice us to whatever god they worship."

"You seem very blasé about what may come, sir."

"After last night, Dragovich," Abdelkrim replied, "I care naught for myself."

They did not have long to wait. Within an hour, the cultists had returned. With them came an older man clad in the same snake-skin robes as the others. With it, he wore a headdress shaped, very roughly, in the likeness of a cobra's head. He strode up to the cages with the air of a man in authority. Abdelkrim instantly knew he must be the leader of the cult. The priest, if that was what he was, completely ignored Dragovich. Instead he went straight to Abelkrim's cage and asked: "Is this the one?" He spoke in Swahili, not the Eritrean tongue. Obviously, he had originated elsewhere in Africa, Abdelkrim considered. It ultimately mattered little to him.

"I speak Swahili fluently, old goat," Abdelkrim snapped in that language. "Kindly refer your words to me rather than your brethren."

"Eh? Eh? The Arabian speaks." The priest cocked his head, evidently much amused.

"I am Persian. My name is Abdelkrim. Learn it well."

"Feh," the old priest replied. "What care I who you are? I care only that you slaughtered many of my tribe."

"We were attacked," Abdelkrim boomed.

"Bah. We are the masters of this land. We are the Children of Yig, and we take what we wish and do what we wish."

Abdelkrim leaned forward, taking the bars in his hands. "Yig?" he said. "I have heard that name. And others. Damballah. Set. Apep. They are all the same to me."

The priest's eyes widened. "What are you saying? You believe in the Almighty Yig?"

Abdelkrim smiled. "I believe in nothing save my own power and destiny. Especially not in your fake gods."

"Blasphemy!" snarled the priest. "You do not believe, yet you dare speak the names of Yig!"

The giant's grin grew wider. "Your words mean nothing to me. I have been touched by Damballah."

At those words, the other cultists stepped back in shock. They began to look at each other, muttering under their breaths. The priest hissed like the snake he worshiped. "Impossible! How can you say this?"

"An old man in Haiti. He told me much."

"No..." the priest's face was incredulous. "No. Not you. He would never touch *you*. You are a pagan, an unbeliever. We are his true worshipers. It is not possible."

Abdelkrim smiled. "If he did not, then how is it I slew so many of your people last night? How is it that I know you cannot slay me now?"

The priest roared. "Enough! I have heard enough blasphemy. You claim to be touched by Yig, foreigner? Bah. We and we alone are the true Children of Yig. But, since you are so certain you are favored by the Mighty One..." He twisted to the others. "Release him! Take him to the riverside. But do not let him go."

Swiftly, Abdelkrim was hauled out of his prison. He would have liked to straighten his back, stretch his limbs, but the cultists had already piled upon him, so many even he could not resist them. They dragged him down to the river and forced him to his knees by the bank. Abdelkrim, grunting, wondered what they were about to do with him. Probably execute him. He had enjoyed playing with these savages' minds a moment ago. Even now he did not believe in what the old man in Haiti had said, although the very fact these fools evidently believed it themselves raised some doubt in his mind. But he did not have time to consider the matter, for the priest was approaching him again.

"Blasphemer, you have claimed favor with Yig and revealed secrets that do not belong to you. You say you are a Child of Damballah, Apep, Set? Very well. As you see, I bear the mark of the Children of Yig on my headdress. Therefore it is only fair that you bear a mark as well, though perhaps not the mark you desire." He held out a hand. "The iron!"

Abdelkrim's eyes opened wide. Placed in the priest's hand was a branding iron, a white-hot thing that scorched just to look at it. The priest, with an evil grin, held it high.

"You who are touched by Yig? Here is your sign!" And he jabbed the iron straight over Abdelkrim's right eye.

It was pain the giant had never felt before. He tore away from his handlers and covered his face with his hands. The priest howled with laughter. Water was splashed over Abdelkrim's face.

"Here, blasphemer!" the priest yelled. "Cool your face." Then he grabbed Abdelkrim and thrust him down head first into the river.

Abdelkrim emerged sputtering and choking. He opened his eyes. By merest chance, he had managed to shut his right eye just before the iron melted into his face. He could still see out of it. His reflection wobbled before him. It was of a bruised, beaten face, exhausted and pale. And, surrounding the right eye like some kind of scarred halo was a mark that resembled nothing so much as the face and hood of a cobra.

SERPENT RISING | **89**

The priest yowled. "Now you look the part of a blasphemer of Yig!" So delighted was he by his cruelty, he broke into a ridiculous little dance, laughing manically.

Abdelkrim stared at his image in the water, stared at the blood-red, burned mark. He felt strength flood his limbs, fueled by a thirst for vengeance. Then he moved like lightning. The cultists were caught completely off guard. Perhaps they felt he would be immobilized with pain. Any ordinary man would have collapsed in agony and despair by this time. But Abdelkrim was by no means ordinary. He would have his revenge.

With a speed that seemed to defy movement, the giant wheeled and seized the priest by his thin legs. Abdelkrim lifted him up, held him upside down as he broke to his feet. Then, before any of the cultists could even move, startled as they obviously were, he thrust the priest head-first into the water. And forced him under. The body in the giant's hands struggled like a fish on a line. Abdelkrim held firm. One of the cultists leaned forward, as if to come to the rescue. Abdelkrim pointed one finger at them all. "Do. Not. Move," was all he said.

None did. The priest thrashed violently, but was utterly unable to escape Abdelkrim's iron grip. Then, the gyrations became weaker, and weaker still. After a few more moments, they ceased entirely. The priest was dead.

Abdelkrim dropped the body into the river. He turned his back on it and faced the cultists. "You saw what I did," he announced. "So, tell me. Would your great Yig have let me accomplish that unless I was a *true* son of his?"

For a long, long moment, there was silence. Then one of the cultists went to his knees. After a moment, another did, then another. One by one the surviving cultists bowed down and paid homage to the man who had slain many of their brethren, and now had proven their priest unworthy.

Abdelkrim accepted their obeisance and pointed to the cage holding Dragovich. "Release him."

They did so. Dragovich came forward, clearly stunned by what had just happened. "I cannot believe this. Wha...what do we do now?"

Abdelkrim gazed once more down at his reflection in the water. The sign of the cobra shone up at him. "We go to Asmara," he stated calmly. "But first, we regroup. And we plan."

* * * * * *

Abdelkrim and his new followers arrived in Asmara at dusk some months later. They walked through the city, ignoring the stares, heading straight for their intended destination–the Governor's Palace, home to Eritrea's president. He had a surprise waiting for him there. All had been pre-arranged.

A large crowd greeted them there, gathered about a platform upon which stood a podium. There, a man in a fine suit—finer than any of his listeners' could afford—spoke into a microphone. Abdelkrim recognized him as the man he wanted to see.

"And I tell you, fellow citizens, that as your president–"

"Cease your prattling," Abdelkrim demanded.

"I–what? Who are you? Where do you come from. Guards. GUARDS!"

Abdelkrim strode forward. Proudly, determinedly, like a living god. "Your guards are no longer yours," he cried out. "They have seen the error of their ways and now follow their true leader." He pushed through the crowd, climbed onto the platform, and moved toward the podium. "As will everyone else."

Abdelkrim's new cult appeared all around the crowd, brandishing weapons of every sort. It was clear who was in control now. "Dragovich!" Abdelkrim cried.

Dragovich tossed a burlap bag onto the platform. Abdelkrim picked it up and withdrew the contents. The crowd collectively gasped. He held the head of the Cobra Cult priest for all to see.

"This man," shouted the giant, "has no power. You feared him as some sort of holy man, or as demon worshipers. I slayed him with my bare hands. He is nothing, was nothing."

"Wha...wha..." was all the president managed to say.

Abdelkrim stepped forward. "I assume power here. Eritrea is now mine."

The president, stunned, quickly realized the reality of the situation, and fell to his knees. "Don't kill me. Please don't kill me."

"Silence!" Abdelkrim sneered. "Your life is in my hands, but...perhaps I can use you. Dragovich. Take him inside the palace. We will talk there."

Dragovich leapt atop the podium and dragged the pleading president away towards to opulent structure.

Abdelkrim then bent over the microphone, facing his new people. "Greetings, my subjects," he began, his voice echoing through the crowd. "You may call me the Cobra."

~ Chapter 8 ~

"At last I had an empire. And my name, my true name. It had only cost the life of my sole friend. Pashmir. How I missed my brother. I still do. I meant the vow I made that day he died. And, for many years, I kept that vow sacrosanct."

"Pashmir...Pashmir..." Khan said blankly.

"I never took a woman for a lover, not even for a night. I was beyond that now. The so-called nobler emotions could no longer sway me. Of that, I was certain. Without my brother, my destiny would be mine alone. On the face of it, it would seem to anyone else that I *had* reached my destiny. I possessed a kingdom, and the rest of the world did not even realize it."

"Kingdom...kingdom..." Khan repeated.

"I had decided, in the end," the Cobra went on, "to listen to my inner voice. I did not declare myself openly. I let the fool Ethiopia had put in place as their puppet remain and made him *my* puppet. To the outside world, I would be known as General Abdelkrim, leader of Eritrea's armed forces, such as they were. But the people of Eritrea knew who I truly was. And they feared me for it."

"Fear...fear..."

"Yes, Khan. I became a master of fear. I traded in it. Dispensed it. Reveled in it. The next few years were busy ones for me. There were rebel groups still extant, fools who refused to acknowledge me as their rightful lord and master. I put them to the sword. Ethiopia, whose government despised me, often sent secret squads in to plunder villages and raise general havoc in my kingdom. I put their heads on spikes. I even had to occasionally deal with the Ayatollah's ridiculous fatwa still against me. Every so often, some zealot from Egypt or Palestine came down to test their mettle against me, to make a name for themselves by besting me. I sent them all to Hell."

"Hell, Master. Hell..."

The Cobra continued his long tale. "Beneath the Governor's Palace, using slave labor, I constructed myself a palace of my own. Underground where no missile or bomb could touch me. A private prison and torture chamber was included in its design. And the world knew nothing of any of this. A few rumors of border skirmishes with neighboring lands, the usual reports of crimes against humanity Eritrea was already known for, that was all. And the world did nothing at all about it. For all their protests against racism and their proclamations of equality for all, in the end most of those who dwell in the modern world care little for blacks in far away lands they've heard nothing about. But not all. And, through these do-gooders, I met the greatest enemy a man could ever have."

* * * * * *

ERITREA - TEN YEARS EARLIER

It was a blazingly hot day. Hot and sticky, the kind of day Abdelkrim—the Cobra—was most used to. But today he sat uncomfortably in the passenger seat of a dusty Jeep, his sweaty fatigues clinging to the hot vinyl like paste. He took a swig of water from his canteen and grimaced at the warm, grimy taste.

The Ethiopians had been acting up again. Raids upon the northern coasts and border country. This time they had been successful enough to overcome tiny villages there, sending refugees fleeing to the south and east. It was usually something his own soldiers could handle themselves, but the Cobra was bored and weary of his rival's constant interference. In truth, he relished the chance for action. He had not had anything like a challenge in some time. The Cobra Cult was destroyed, its members dead or scattered. The last of the rebels had joined them in death or banishment. The only thing remaining was to locate, if possible, this Disciple of the Mountains the old man of Haiti had told him to seek out.

He had agents pouring over the country questioning, interrogating, and occasionally torturing villagers from the remotest parts for information, but they had returned with nothing. Either the natives held this Disciple in such awe they absolutely would not speak of him, or the man simply did not exist. Eventually, all he managed to ascertain was that, if this Disciple did exist, he would surely be found atop the holy peak of Emba Soira. Surely? He wondered at that, wondered if the old man had merely been playing him for a fool, or was simply just an old fool himself. Either way, he had to know for sure. Even though he now possessed an empire, he wanted more. Much more. It was his destiny.

The Cobra sighed. He was hot and frustrated. He missed Pashmir. He had been thinking of commissioning some kind of memorial to his brother, but could not decide just what it should be. Perhaps some sort of statue.... He glanced around at the small troop he had gathered to deal with the insurgents. Dragovich was there, looking over some maps, discussing plans with the men. A loyal man, the Cobra mulled. It was hard to find such these days.

The radio buzzed, and his driver lifted the mike. The Cobra tuned the words out, his mind still focused on the future tribute to his brother. Then the driver faced him.

"General Abdelkrim! I mean–Master!"

The Cobra came out of his reverie. "What is it?"

"Reports of a Red Cross camp some miles from here. They're feeding and medicating the refugees."

"What!" the Cobra sat rigidly in his seat. "I forbade them entry into the country months ago. None may offer succor to my people without my permission. How long has the Red Cross been encamped?"

The driver shrugged. "Master, I do not–"

The Cobra slammed a fist into his driver's face. "Imbecile!" Then he tossed him out of his seat. "You!" he pointed to another soldier. "Come here. You are now my driver. We go to this camp. And–you, you, you" –he began pointing to soldiers at random– "you all accompany me. Bring your weapons. Dragovich! Take the rest of the men and engage the enemy. I want no survivors."

"Sir," Dragovich began. "I would rather go with y–"

"Obey my commands," the Cobra shouted. "The rest of you–come with me."

* * * * * *

"It was a typical refugee camp, Khan," the Cobra said within the dank asylum cell. "Small and wretched, filled with the sick and starving. Pathetic. A worthless collection of cowardly sheep that would have been better off if the Ethiopians had killed them. I saw the Red Cross trucks through my binoculars. I ordered our platoon to enter the camp. As we drove within I saw a ragtag collection of westerners, mainly white, moving in and out of a field of emaciated black skeletons. Some were cleansing boils and sores on the wounded, others were offering soup and bread to the starving. Even in that rabble, two westerners in particular stood out. The first was a black woman, tall, lovely. She stood and walked with an air of determination and dignity I rarely saw in a female. Though black I heard her speak and realized she was an American."

"American, Master. Infidels," Khan whispered.

"The second was an American, also. A white male. Handsome, I suppose, but the moment I saw him I knew he was soft. Decadent. The product of a life of privilege and luxury he had not earned. He did not look as if he belonged there. Very probably his presence there was meant as some fashionable fad–go help some starving Africans. He clearly never worked a day in his life. I dismissed him instantly as a man of no consequence. How could such a weak man possibly threaten the Cobra?"

"Weak man...weak man..."

"It was the sole mistake of my life, Khan. My one error of judgment."

* * * * * *

ERITREA - TEN YEARS EARLIER

"We're in trouble, Paul," the Cobra heard the black woman say as he leapt out of the Jeep. "That's General Abdelkrim. He's supposed to be the head of the Army, though rumor says he's the absolute dictator of the country."

"I *am* absolute dictator of this country, woman," the Cobra snapped as his men lined up behind him, rifles pointed. "And you have been warned about setting up camp in this area. We do not condone your presence here."

The black woman snorted, stamping her foot. "You have no right to stop us. We're a legally sanctioned international aid agency. We're only here to help feed and medicate the sick and starving. We have no interest in your stupid border war."

The white man–Paul–had stood by, watching with a stupid look on his face, saying nothing. The Cobra glanced at him, and smirked. As he thought, a weakling. So cowardly he had to let a woman do all the talking.

"Perhaps not," the Cobra snarled in reply, "but I have an interest in you. I ordered you not to come here. Now you shall be taught to respect my authority."

The woman stepped forward, her features etched in fury. "If you think for one minute I'm going to let you–"

"Silence!" the Cobra roared. He pointed a finger at her. One of the Cobra's men stepped forward. The crack of a bullet, and a single red hole appeared in the woman's head. She sagged at the knees, eyes wide, and fell to the ground dead.

It seemed to goad Paul into action. "Judy!" he cried, darting forward. Blood streamed from the horrendous wound. The man carefully cradled her in his arms. "Judy–oh God! Judy...no. No, Judy, no!" Around him the other westerners stood stock-still, too stunned to move. Neither did anyone else.

"Her life was forfeit. None may challenge my authority," the Cobra said.

"You sonnuva..." Paul started. In an instant, he was upon his feet, charging the Cobra. "I'm going to kill you."

"Infidel!" the Cobra roared, sending his left arm out in a great, sweeping curve. "You dare try to touch me?"

Paul went flying. The Cobra could see the blood spurt from the man's nose and lips as he slammed into the ground with a thud. The sight brought him great satisfaction. This Paul, whomever he was, was nothing. Less than nothing.

The Cobra whipped around. He snapped his gaze toward the ragged, emaciated forms of the gathered refugees who had dared come to this camp seeking succor. Scrawny, skeletal peons who had forgotten whom their master was. Already they were stepping back from his presence, pulling their children behind them. Shields of skin-and-bone to protect their loved ones. It would not be enough. The Cobra flicked a finger. Behind him, sharp *snik* of automatic weapons being readied. He pointed toward the refugees and their tents.

The barrage was deafening.

Idly, the Cobra snuffed a wisp of grey smoke snaking toward his nose away. "Gather the bodies in a pile and burn them. Ensure the plume is seen for mi–" The sight of Paul, crawling back to his feet, caused the Cobra to halt in his tracks. Did this fool not know when to stay down?

Paul was rising, pulling himself up from his bloodied puddle in the grime. And he smiled. It was a smile the Cobra was well familiar with. And shook him to his core, as the memories from his childhood came back to him in an instant. Paul's legs shook like fragile trees in the wind as he stumbled upward, his face was dyed black from the Cobra's blow. But he still rose to his full height.

"I'll kill you," Paul said again.

Their eyes met, and the Cobra thought for a moment he saw something. The smile, yes, but there was something else as well. A fierce will to live, a thirst for vengeance, perhaps even...a being of destiny? Like himself? Before the Cobra could make sense of his thoughts, one of his men lifted his Heckler and Koch MP5 butt outward. Paul didn't see him until it was too late. The butt slashed forward, slamming into the side of Paul's head. This time he did not get up.

The soldier's face was flush with glee. The Cobra knew the type–young and conceited, filled with a sense of power now that he wore a uniform and held a rifle in his hand. A bloodthirsty smirk upon his face, the soldier twisted the sub-machine gun around to finish the job.

"Wait," the Cobra found himself ordering.

What am I doing? the Cobra thought.

The soldier paid no attention. He had tasted blood today and yearned for more. A thin finger began to clench the trigger.

The Cobra's hand dropped to his belt. The air whistled as a streak of silver flashed through the sky. A geyser of crimson spurted as the tip of the knife buried itself deep into the tender flesh of the soldier's throat. "I said wait!"

The young soldier's eyes bulged frog-like with disbelief as he briefly watched his own lifeblood spill. Then, with a low, mournful moan, he fell forward and joined the American in the dust. Neither moved. Nor did the other soldiers, who clearly knew better to follow orders.

The Cobra strode forward. Ignoring the corpse of his soldier, he instead knelt and turned over Paul's prone body. He felt for a pulse. There, very faint and whispery, the slightest beat. The American was yet alive. The Cobra let the prone form sink back to the earth. He stood, brushing the dust from his uniform. He knew why he had reacted earlier, realized why he had saved the American's life. For a brief moment, when their eyes had locked, as Paul smiled, he saw something he recognized. Something, or someone, he knew all too well–himself. For that brief moment, it was almost as though the Cobra had been looking in a mirror. And in that moment, he couldn't–*could not*–let *himself* die.

"Burn the camp," he ordered finally. "Leave nothing and no one behind. Ensure the plume is seen for miles. I want the world to know what happened here today. I want it to know the Cobra's will is law, without fail, without exception."

Coughing self-consciously, one of the soldier's finally found the courage to speak. "And this one?" he pointed to the American, Paul.

Slowly a grim smile crossed the Cobra's face. Perhaps he could not kill this...Paul, for whatever quirk of his mind–or Fate?–prevented him from doing so, but that didn't mean he had to let him live. "No. Do not kill him. We will take him with us. Then dump him in the middle of the Danikil Depression. An infidel such as he will not last the day in that region."

He watched with satisfaction as his men began their grim work. As a couple dumped Paul into the back of the Jeep, he hopped into his seat and directed the driver to move out. The Jeep backed up to pull out of the camp, while the Cobra looked back at the unconscious American and the words of the old man in Haiti came back to him.

You shall be opposed. Opposed by one equal to you. He shall trail you, always, like an invisible wraith in the night. The battle between life and light, death and darkness shall be fought between you. But only one can emerge the victor. You will know them when they remind you of your childhood.

An opponent. An opponent of equal worth to him. To be known when he reminded the Cobra of himself. The thought–realization?–hit him like a jackhammer.

The American? This...Paul? Equal to me? No. No. A thousand times no.

It was impossible. He was the Cobra, and this fool was nothing more than a decadent infidel. It could not be true. *Was* not true.

And that was the last time the Cobra considered the matter.

* * * * * *

"But it was not the last time, Khan," the Cobra said wistfully. The old man had been correct all along. The American's full name was Paul Sanderson. I looked at his identification. The name meant nothing to me then. We dumped him on a dune in the middle of the Danikil Depresssion. That is a landscape in the Afar region of Ethiopia, near the Eritrean border. The Ethiopians are not the only ones who cross lines illegally. It is also the hottest place on Earth. Rain never falls there. Temperatures can reach one hundred twenty-five degrees. Without water or shelter, no man can survive more than a few days."

"Water...water..." Khan stammered.

"I knew the American would not last," the Cobra continued, ignoring his henchman. "So, we left him. Yes, we left him there alive. As I said before, for some reason I still do not fully comprehend, I did not kill Sanderson there and then. But I was determined he should die all the same. And I dismissed him from my mind. Within days I had forgotten the entire incident. Dragovich came back having driven the interlopers away, and my life returned to normal."

"Normal...normal..."

"Then from a long trip into the interior, one of my agents returned. What he had to report would change my life forever. But not quite as I had hoped or expected. And it bequeathed me a lifelong enemy. One which I will soon vanquish, Khan."

~ Chapter 9 ~

ERITREA - YEARS EARLIER

"You are certain of this?" the Cobra studied the map skeptically.

"Yes, Master," the agent said. "It took days, but he finally talked. He said it was here" –he jabbed a finger at a particular point on the large, unfolded map upon the desk– "that the Disciple could be found."

"Mmm," the Cobra said, thinking intently. His eyes narrowed as he regarded the circled area. "A difficult climb?"

"Yes, Master. Most difficult and hazardous conditions."

A group of six men converged in the Cobra's private office–Mikhail Dragovich, and four agents who served as spies and secret police, all faced their lord and master. One man in particular was the subject of the Cobra's attention. He had brought news that interested the warlord greatly.

"There can be no mistake, Master," the agent insisted. "The peak of Emba Soira. He was most insistent. In my view...the man you seek can be nowhere else."

"I see," the Cobra said, not really sure what to believe. "That does tally with the rumors we heard previously. You are certain this man spoke the truth?"

"As certain I can be, Master. I tortured him for days. I slaughtered his son in front of him. In the end, he despaired. I promised I would kill him quickly if he finally told the truth. He did. I know it."

"*I* must know it," the Cobra replied harshly. "Your own life depends upon it." The agent appeared flustered for a moment, but held his ground. The Cobra rolled up the map with a snap, and tossed it aside. "Enough. Dragovich. Prepare my camping gear, and enough supplies to last me ten days. I go to this mountain to see what is there. I go alone."

"If I may, sir," Dragovich murmured, "Are you sure that is wise?"

The Cobra's eyes narrowed. "Are you questioning me?"

"No, sir," Dragovich hastened to answer. "Just this man. How do we really know this Disciple of the Mountain isn't anything more than a myth? I say he *is* myth. Some guru sitting in his cave high on a mountaintop. It's like one of those American novels or fairy tales. Foolishness."

"I tortured the man–" the agent began.

"Feh. I've tortured men, too, back in the Russian Army. In the end, they would say anything they thought their torturer wanted to hear, just to make the pain stop. You cannot believe a story based on that."

"I do not base it on just that," the Cobra snapped. "I base it on something you could not possibly begin to understand." The Cobra turned to his loyal lieutenant. "There is something in what you say, but...I *must* know the truth. I *must* know, and the power promised me *must* be mine. Now, carry out my orders. I go to this mountain alone. And if there is power there for me to claim–I shall."

* * * * * *

"After a long journey merely to reach the mountains, I wandered them for days thereafter, Khan. At last I had found potential evidence for what I had long sought. If there truly was a Disciple of the Mountain, I would find him–and I would bend him to my will. I would take whatever knowledge and power he possessed and claim it as my own. It was my destiny."

Khan swayed to and fro while the Cobra spoke.

"At long last, with my provisions exhausted and my strength flagging, I came across a timber dwelling at the very peak–a narrow plateau–of Emba Soira. This had to be it. My destiny awaited."

* * * * * *

ERITREA - YEARS EARLIER

The Cobra looked at the hut in disbelief. This could not be what he had sought for so long. It simply could not. A simple hut. Made of wood and mud, just like a thousand others he had seen before. Not a majestic temple dedicated to some ancient, forgotten god, nor a grand mansion. Just a hut. It made no sense to him. Yet–this was it. It *had* to be. The final step on the long, tortured path to his destiny. If his vision was to come true at all...it had to happen here. He took a deep breath. He had no idea what he would find inside. But he was determined to find out and, despite his exhaustion, he would wait no longer.

He strode to the door. It was closed against him, a thing of heavy wood. He charged, slamming into it with a massive shoulder. It cracked but didn't budge. Undeterred, he stepped several paces back, and charged again. With a grunt of triumph, it snapped upon its hinges, flying open. The Cobra eagerly stepped inside. And was shocked by what he witnessed.

Two figures sat before him. One was an ancient man–as ancient as the old man in Haiti. Like that one, he was bald, bearded and as wizened as an over-dried fig. He sat cross-legged upon the floor, holding, again like the Haitian, a long stick serving as a cane in his hand. It was the other figure, however, that astonished the Cobra with his presence. He had changed dramatically since the Cobra had last seen him. As he stood at the titan's intrusion, the Cobra could see he was more muscular now. More powerful. The years of soft living he must have experienced in America had fallen away. His air was different: more forceful, more confident. And his eyes, when they met, seemed to gleam with a power the Cobra could not fathom.

It was him. The American. Sanderson. "You!"

Sanderson launched himself at the Cobra with a cry of anger and vengeance. Whatever change had happened to the man, whatever power he had acquired, he clearly had not yet mastered them. With a backward punch, the Cobra sent Sanderson sprawling. The American hit the crude wall of the hut, making the entire building tremble.

The Cobra snorted. "I know not how you escaped with your life. I was obviously too merciful with you. I shall not make that mistake again."

SERPENT RISING | **107**

Sanderson struggled to his feet, shaken. The Cobra turned his attention to the old man. He was surprised to find the man had risen from his position without making a sound. He simply stared at the Cobra as if he were some interesting animal in a cage.

"You're coming here was foreseen," the old man said simply. "But you are too late. The secrets of the scriptures will remain forever hidden from you." The old man chuckled a bit, as if amused by some secret joke.

The Cobra felt a fury engulf his body. "Then I have no further use for you!" *If this old fool will not give his secrets to me, then he will give them to no one.* The Cobra drew back his arm and lashed out with a massive fist. Like Sanderson, the Disciple of the Mountain slammed against the wall. He slumped down and did not move.

In an instant, Sanderson was at the old man's side. Swiftly, he knelt and checked for a pulse.

The Cobra smirked. "He is finished. A fate you will now share."

Slowly, the man named Sanderson rose to his feet. Then he looked at the Cobra with even more hate than he had exhibited when the woman had been slain months previous. "Not this day," he said. Then the battle truly began.

The two met in a clash of blows. The Cobra was surprised. The American *was* stronger than he had been before. Now that he was prepared, he stood his ground as the Cobra sent strike after strike into his face and chest. Sanderson struck back hard as well. Though the Cobra was by far the taller man, Sanderson had courage and anger on his side. Again and again he slammed into the warlord, punching, pummeling, beating with all his might. As he did, the Cobra felt something odd. A kind of crackle in the air, like some kind of electrical activity. It grew as Sanderson kept up the attack.

The Cobra shot a glance at the American's face. Sanderson had the same determination, the same belief in his own destiny, in his eyes, as the Cobra held for his. Sanderson flashed a brief smile at his enemy. They truly were more alike than the Cobra cared to admit. The eerie energy in the atmosphere seemed to grow. To his horror, the Cobra realized the truth of the matter. It was the power. Whatever power the old man was supposed to have had, he had somehow transferred it, given it away. To *this* man. This infidel, this fool who dared believe himself equal to the Cobra. It was *inside* Sanderson, crackling, flowing. Empowering him to fight on when he should have fallen.

No. The power is mine. Mine!

With a roar of rage, the Cobra let forth in even greater intensity. Whatever power Sanderson now possessed, it was clear he was still the inferior in experience and skill. The Cobra would yet prove victorious. He slammed Sanderson over the head with both fists, sending him to the floor once more. The American rolled over, his face a pulp of black bruises. "I grow weary of this. Let us finish this."

"Let's," shrieked Sanderson. With a last burst of strength, he shot to his feet and swung his arm.

The Cobra had not seen the chunk of wood that had been lying by the fallen American. Now Sanderson threw it, aiming directly for the warlord's face. The timber made contact right over his right eye. "ARRRRRGHHH!" the Cobra screamed. He staggered back, hands over his face. Still screaming, he pulled his hands away and lifted his head. From where his right eye had been the thick splinter jutted out, sending blood streaming from the socket. "You gnat! I will crush you like the bug you are!" With a howl of rage, the

Cobra rushed forward, and snatched Sanderson up in a bear hug before he could move. With all the strength he possessed, he began to squeeze. Sanderson struggled but the pressure against his lungs grew more and more intense. Through the blood and pain the Cobra smiled. Smiled the same way he had as a child, the same way he had always done. "Die," he hissed.

Then it happened. The energy burst.

The air that had been crackling a moment earlier suddenly surged in intensity. Then, from nowhere–no, from Sanderson–the light came. It erupted forth like a spewing volcano, its energy a blinding, pulsating, living thing. It did not flow, it *deluged*, blasting the Cobra off his feet, breaking his hold on Sanderson. It was blazing, searing, and it washed across both men. They jerked back, barely able to keep their balance. Sanderson seemed as awestruck as the Cobra at the electrical blast. He stood there with mouth agape, evidently dumbfounded with what was emerging from his own body.

The Cobra howled in pain. "I–unnnhh–know now how you are capable of this...but I shall not–ahhh–fall to the likes of you!" With every ounce of strength left, he plunged toward his foe. It was like pushing through a physical barrier. But he would not be halted. Bit by bit he forced himself through the energy burst. The power was...*increasing*. It felt like being trapped in an electrical generator gone wild, losing more and more control over itself. The Cobra inched forward, however, determined to kill his damned foe.

Sanderson seemed to wake from his trance and leapt for the warlord. The Cobra reached for Sanderson, Sanderson reached for him. They seized hold of each other in a wrestler's grapple. Before either could continue the battle, the light jerked into even higher gear. A mass of it seemed to congeal about the Cobra's head. His right eye, still bleeding profusely from the splinter therein, started to smoke. The splinter fell, a black and charred thing. And his eye suddenly took on the glow of the surrounding energy, turning a milky white.

"What–what are you doing to me? I feel..feel a power building inside me," the Cobra uttered. Sanderson said nothing. Possibly even he did not know what was happening there and then. But the warlord's insides were burning with an incredible heat as if every organ had been torched. He convulsed once, twice. "What is happening?" he gasped aloud. Then he screamed. So did Sanderson. The white-hot electrical energy flowing madly around them had hit critical mass. It could take no more. It was like being caught in a supernova.

An explosion tore through the structure. Then...nothing.

The Cobra awoke with his entire body feeling as if it had been torn apart atom by atom. For a second he could not remember where he was. The sky reeled about him. The explosion had torn the roof off. His mind was reeling. He could not concentrate. How long had he been out? He did not know. The only thing he could think of was one thing– retreat. Leave. Abandon that place and leave whomever and whatever might remain behind to their fate.

Somehow, he staggered to his feet. He was only vaguely aware of the presence of what seemed to be two bodies also lying nearby. But he could not quite remember who they were or why they were there, so he ignored them. He had to leave. Escape. That was all that mattered.

It was the only thing that mattered.

* * * * * *

"It was not until I was well down the mountain that my senses finally came back to me, Khan. I remembered the battle, the incredible energy–and I realized something else. That power, the power the old man had guarded, the power that flowed through Sanderson...now flowed through me. Somehow, in that last grapple, the American transferred some of it into my own body. Only a portion of it, to be sure, which galls me to this day. But portion or not, I now had the power I had always yearned for, and I no longer shared with humanity the one aspect of it I hated most. Its frailty."

~ Chapter 10 ~

"Power, Khan. At last I had...true power. Though only some of what should have been completely mine–and mine alone–I finally had what I always desired. That which was my destiny!"

"Destiny...destiny..." Khan mumbled.

"Yes, Khan. I had become more than human. Whatever ancient science or magic the Disciple had guarded was now at least partially mine to command. I believed Sanderson to have perished in the explosion. That suited me well. Now, no other shared the power that flowed through me. All that remained was to gain absolute control of my newfound abilities."

"Master...Master..."

"I returned to Asmara in triumph. As the days passed, I learned the exact nature of those abilities. My strength and stamina had been increased, albeit only slightly. My aging was retarded, so I look younger now than I truly am. But most spectacular of all, I found that I was able to dominate men's minds. Not by physical force or strength of personality, but by sheer will. Within my right eye lies the ability to hypnotize others, conquer their souls, make them my slaves, or to influence their moods or shield me from their sight. Naturally, I began making use of it right away."

"But Master...Master..." Khan begged, though the Cobra could only guess if he actually had something he wanted to say.

"Silence, Khan! I mesmerized several of my followers whom I felt were not as loyal to me as they should have been. I cemented the obedience of the government of Eritrea. Ironically, I did not bother to seize the mind of Dragovich-his loyalty to me was beyond question. But others I did, and their service to me became all the greater as a result. Soon, however, Eritrea became too small for me. At long last I understood the prophecy the old man in Haiti had given me."

"Old man...old man..."

"I began to travel again," the Cobra pressed on. "Visiting old acquaintances in the criminal and terrorist underworlds. And I captured their minds. Not of every member, you understand, merely the top echelons. They became my slaves. The world thought they were all independent of each other, but I began to forge them into an army that served only me. I forged new alliances as well. Traveled to lands previously unknown to me. That is how I met you, Khan. As it turned out, you offered your loyalty to me freely, of your own will. And I took it. You became one of my highest officers. Slowly, but inexorably, my empire was growing. My vision of years long past was finally coming to pass. But I still had bumps to overcome. One of those bumps proved to be Mikhail Dragovich."

FRANK DIRSCHERL & GREG GICK

* * * * * *

ERITREA - YEARS EARLIER

"Bring him," the Cobra said as he sat upon his throne in stately judgment.

A crime had been committed and it was time for justice. He had eschewed his former military fatigues as unworthy of him now. Today he sat in regal splendor in a costume he felt befitted his innate majesty more. He clad his giant frame in a form-fitting garment of blood-red; silken and without wrinkle. Heavy black boots shod his feet. A cape of the same black flowed down from his massive shoulders. In it he looked no longer the titan–he looked the god. Which was precisely what he knew himself to be–a god upon earth.

The place was a special hall in Asmara set aside for his specific judgments. The people of Eritrea did not know of its existence, it was essentially his throne room, where the Cobra presided over his kingdom.

"Bring him," the Cobra said again.

"Yes, Master," Magnus Khan, the Cobra's newest recruit, hastened to obey. The Mongolian Hahn had proven himself a loyal and obedient servant. He had once been a third-rate bandit chief eking out an existence plundering remote villages that weren't worth the trouble. It had been a terrible winter when the Cobra had encountered Khan. He and his band had been slowly starving to death, which made them all the more desperate in their raids. The Cobra had never told Khan why he was in Mongolia at that time of year. But when he had charged the giant with his horse in the middle of that snow-buried plain, the Cobra had taken him down with little effort. That was when Khan had pledged eternal loyalty to the Cobra. No other option existed for him.

Khan and another slave dragged the prisoner inside. The man was clasped in chains from head to foot and had to be shoved along just to enable him to move along the floor. The prisoner struggled all the way, but it was to no avail. Within moments he was standing before the Cobra, defiance shining in his eyes.

"Dragovich. Mikhail," the Cobra greeted softly.

Mikhail Dragovich was slammed in the back by a rod, forcing him to his knees.

"Oh, Mikhail, Mikhail," the Cobra sighed. "You are my biggest disappointment. After years of loyal service, I discover you to be a spy. That you have been feeding information to the Russians for years. I believed in your loyalty. But you have betrayed me."

"Go to hell!" Dragovich spat through his teeth.

The Cobra shook his head. "I know who you really are, Piotr Blackov. I have spies, too. They have told me everything."

"I serve the People of the Soviet Union," snarled Blackov.

"Unchain him!" Instantly, Khan and the other man began working on Blackov's shackles.

The moment he was free, Blackov stood, glared at the Cobra with hate burning in his eyes. "I serve the People," he said again. "I shall never betray them. I would give my life for them."

"They have betrayed you," the Cobra began. "I assure you, you shall not be missed by them. But it scarcely matters anymore. Here." The Cobra tossed a knife across the floor. "Kill yourself."

Blackov did not move. "I shall not."

"Oh, but you will." The white marble of the Cobra's right eye suddenly burst into life. Blackov tried to flinch away, but Khan forced his head toward it, pried his eyes open. "Look at me, Blackov," the Cobra commanded. "Look at me and pick up that knife."

"Nuh...nuh–" Blackov grit his teeth as he tried to resist. The gleam grew even brighter. His will visibly slipped away.

"Take–up–your–knife," the Cobra ordered again.

Slowly Blackov sank back to the floor and reached out a hand. His finger entwined along the handle of the blade.

"And now kill yourself. For the People. For *me!*"

"Nnn..*NNNNNN–*"

"*DO IT!*"

"For the People!" Blackov screamed and plunged the blade directly into his heart.

The Cobra leaned back in his throne as Blackov's body sagged to the floor. "He is dead, Master," Khan said. "What shall we do with him?"

"Cut off the head and burn the body," the Cobra said, rising to leave. He pushed his way past his slaves and headed for the door to his own quarters. "Then send it to the Kremlin. They can have the traitor."

* * * * * *

MOSCOW - YEARS EARLIER

It was a double funeral that frigid winter in Moscow. The mourners gathered about the graveside to say their final goodbyes. The faceless man stood near the back, as unobtrusive and unnoticeable as ever.

Elisabet Blackova had collapsed the day he had come to tell her the news. She had died the next day. Grief, the doctors told him. Strange. All these years, and she had never stopped hoping for her husband's return. Piotr Blackov must have been a better man than he thought, the faceless man pondered. But what could he do? The State had its needs, and the life of one man was of secondary importance.

He had kept his promise. He had seen to Elisbet and her daughter's well-being ever since sending Blackov away. He knew Natalya had never forgiven him that action. But she would learn. There she was now. Older and showing even more beauty than her mother. She stood alone by the graves, head down, though she was not weeping. That was good. That meant she was learning. That meant she could be used.

The faceless man cornered her alone as soon as he could. "My sincere condolences for your loss, my dear." Natalya said nothing. She hated him, he knew. But still he was determined to recruit her. "The Cobra is a madman. He needs to be brought down."

Natalya looked up, sniffing, and nodded. "Yes," was all she whispered.

"I can help you with that, Natalya. I have helped you before, and I can help you again. You could have your revenge."

The girl looked at him askance. He could read the suspicion in her eyes. "How?" she finally said.

"Come to work for me. You are alone, have nowhere else to go. I can teach you how to avenge your parents' death. But you must come to work for me. There is no other way."

"Doing what my father did?"

The faceless man did not deny it. "Yes."

Natalya Blackova was silent a very long time. She turned away from him, thinking. He watched her in silence. Then, at last, she turned to face him again, a new determination in her eyes. "Yes," was all she said.

"Then come along," he said, and she followed.

The faceless man briefly wondered if, perhaps, he was inviting trouble upon himself by recruiting Natalya, but those thoughts quickly drifted away as they strode through the cold winter morning...

* * * * * *

"Natalya. My Natalya. I had sworn I would never love. I had sworn no one could ever touch my heart after Pashmir died."

"Love...love..." Khan muttered.

"Even the Cobra can be mistaken."

~ Chapter 11 ~

MOSCOW - YEARS EARLIER

The faceless man had been staring out the window at the street below, observing the crowds gathered in Red Square. He grimaced at what he saw. Thousands of young people chanting, waving flags, demanding change. He glanced at the issue of Pravda upon his desk. The headlines read of mobs, discontent, breakaways.

Disgusting. In the old days rebels like this would have been shot in the streets. Tanks would have rolled over them. At least the Chinese had gotten that right in Tianamen Square.

But things were changing now, faster than he could keep track of them. The Berlin Wall had fallen. East Germany was no more. Poland was lost. And now this. There were morbid forecasts that the Union would not last more than another month under such conditions. Perhaps not even a week. Several of his cronies were already draining their secret caches to beat a hasty retreat if necessary.

Perhaps he should, too. The faceless man prided himself on his survival skills. He had come through Stalingrad, Stalin's purges and more by knowing what palms to grease, what favors to ask and bestow, and who to sacrifice. Many had fallen so he could live. That was the way it was in a materialistic universe. Survival of the fittest. Winner take all. And know when to leave the game. He had enough in the Swiss account not even his superiors knew of. Perhaps it was time–

"He is in Eritrea!" Natalya Blackova's face was a storm of rage as she burst into the door.

Damn, I thought I'd locked that.

"What are you asking of me, Natalya?"

"The Cobra, damn you! The murderer of my parents. He's been back in Eritrea for weeks."

"I suppose he has," the faceless man replied calmly. "What do you want me to do about it?"

"About it? About it! I want you to send me there. I want you to let me kill the man you promised I could."

"Natayla, Natalya, look around you," the faceless man beckoned out the window. "Our country is disintegrating before our very eyes. We are fighting to save our very way of life, and you wish to break away simply to fulfill a stupid vendetta?"

"Stupid? Stupid!" she was furious now.

The faceless man snorted. "Natalya...you have trained well these past months, it is true, but you are not yet ready for a man such as the Cobra. He is...monstrous, he is...inhuman." He shuffled around to face her. "No, your place is here for the time being. The People need you. *I* need you."

To be my patsy as I make my escape, he thought.

"Now, report to headquarters. I shall have orders for you soon."

And he pushed past her and made his way to the door.

* * * * * *

Natalya, her fury unabated, picked up the phone on the sole desk in the room and dialed. "Hello. Is this the airport? Get me a flight to North Africa."

~ Chapter 12 ~

ERITREA - YEARS EARLIER

"Do you like it, Master?"

The sculpture shone in the sun with a blinding golden glare, as if emitting a powerful glow all its own. Onyx of the purest cut and clarity flashed with a midnight black, while diamond fangs and claws refracted the light like white flame. The emerald eyes glowed as though alive.

The statue of the leopard leaping upon its prey raised above all their heads, even the Cobra's. Upon the bronze pedestal, a gleaming gold plate with raised letters boldly stated:

PASHMIR
NOBLEST OF BROTHERS - I SHALL NOT FORGET

SERPENT RISING | 123

The small crowd gathered about the statute murmured their approval. In any other land, this effigy would be immortalized in the history of art, the Cobra felt sure. It was magnificent. Every museum in the world, had they known of its existence, should battle each other for the honor of housing it within their walls.

That sculptress once was a struggling art student in New York City, brilliant but ignored thanks to a lack of patrons and principal. But the Cobra admired her skills. It had been the work of a child to corner her one night as she returned home and expose her to his will. Now she was a loyal servant who had slaved for months to create the greatest tribute to the first and only friend of the greatest man in the world. The Cobra was well pleased.

"Do you like it, Master?" she asked again, blank-faced but sounding concerned. She had no desire other than to please the Cobra, as he well knew. No idea or intention entered her head other than to make him happy. His will commanded it thus.

The Cobra said nothing. He was examining the work with contemplative eyes. At long last, he finished his inspection and nodded. "Excellent. A fitting tribute to my brother. You have done well, my dear."

The sculptress bowed. "I live to serve my master."

"Of course you do." Once more the Cobra turned his attention from his slave to the sculpture. A small part of him wondered what to do with the woman now. She had served her purpose and he no longer needed her. She was rather pretty, he supposed, though that was hardly of import to him, and he had overheard one of his men expressing an interest in her. Perhaps he'd turn her over to him as a wife?

Wife. Companion. Friend.

The Cobra had none of those. He had slaves, lackeys, minions. Nothing else. Nor did he want anything more. When Pashmir had died, he had sworn in his heart to never let anyone into it again. Thus far he had kept that vow. He could envision no circumstance to ever change it. While he was pleased with the memorial, pleased with his abilities and power, he was yet unfulfilled. Eritrea now felt restricting for him. He wanted more, much more. His destiny demanded it. But where next? And how? When?

Lost in his thoughts, the Cobra almost missed the scream of danger in his head. Normally his instincts were a finely-honed tool, alerting him to any threat. This time it was an annoying fly that saved his life. The creature was buzzing irksomely in his ear and automatically he raised a hand to swat it, angling his head slightly for a better sight of its pinwheel flight. That is when, out of the corner of his eye, he saw the refraction of light off metal, and instantly knew what it was.

"Down!" he roared, shoving Khan to the ground with one hand even as the sharp *sheeek* of an automatic rifle burst whistled forth. In the next moment, he seized the sculptress and hauled her before his own body. She suddenly gave a convulsive jerk as a bullet exploded through her sternum. She gurgled, then breathed her last. The Cobra threw the body aside. He had no regrets or even thought about her use as a human shield. Like everyone else, she existed only to serve him, in life...or death. Magnus Khan, his loyal lieutenant, was worth saving. She was not.

Everyone else had hit the dirt the moment the shot was fired. The Cobra ignored them. He plunged forth swiftly in the direction the bullet had come, a clump of yellowing but still thick brush. He knew that at any moment yet another bullet might issue forth, but he was counting that an unexpected charge, rather than fleeing the scene, would confound his would-be assassin. Regardless, the Cobra had never run from a battle. Never.

His plan worked. He caught a glimpse of black from the brush as it flashed away. The Cobra pounded after it, crashing through the foliage with the speed and energy of an enraged rhinoceros. He paused just long enough at the site the shooter had initially hidden away to see the abandoned rifle flung onto the ground. SV-98, he recognized. Soviet.

Once more he caught a flash of black in the distance and took off after it. The assassin, whomever it was, was a swift one. But the Cobra was faster. Within seconds, he had halved the distance between them, then quickly halved it again. He was certain his attacker was headed for a small gathering of date trees only a few dozen yards ahead. He would not let them escape. The Cobra increased his speed. Now he was within the grove, eyes flashing in every direction. No sign of his foe. The grove was empty save for a few startled birds already taking to wing. The assassin could not have gone far. So where had he–

The Cobra sensed the presence dropping from above just before it struck and cursed himself for an imbecile. *The trees, of course.* The gigantic warlord's razor-sharp reflexes allowed him just enough time to prepare himself for the impact. If he had not, his neck likely would have snapped. He felt the assassin slam upon his back, sensed two long legs whip around his torso and interlock themselves. Peripheral vision caught two black-clad hands flash around on either side of his neck. Then something was pressing into his flesh. Barbed wire? He felt pressure drawing his neck back, felt blood drip down, his air was being cut off. He was being garroted.

Instinct screamed for the Cobra to seize the wire and try to yank it away. But his enemy's grip was too tight. He would asphyxiate before he could free himself that way. Instead, his hands shot down, grasped the ends of his cape. Swiftly he hauled it up, over his head and over the head of his would-be killer. The unexpected action startled his attacker enough for the pressure upon his throat to give, just a little. It was enough. With a roar, the Cobra jerked his entire torso forward in a long sweeping bow. At the same time he removed his cape, and tossed it aside. The combination of actions was enough to cause the assassin to lose his grip around the Cobra's waist. He fell backward. The Cobra expected the figure would go down hard and he could then pin him to earth. He was wrong. To the Cobra's surprise, the assassin somersaulted in midair, rolling his body to land upon his feet, who then whirled to face him. Before him stood, ready to charge again, a figure indeed dressed in all black from boots to the ski-mask covering their head. Nothing could hide, however, the slender, distinctly feminine form that outfit covered.

"Murderer!" the female cried in Russian and leapt for him.

The Cobra flashed out an arm in an attempt to swat her aside. The woman caught his arm, and pulled with all her strength. The Cobra lost his balance as his shoulder nearly dislocated itself. He went down to one knee and a black boot connected with his chin.

"You killed my father! My mother!" his attacker screamed. "Now you die."

"I think not," the Cobra snapped. He was tiring of this game. The blow to his face hurt. He had not suffered an injury like that since...since the American Sanderson. Swiftly he interlocked his fingers, bringing both hands up in an arc like an oversized fist. They connected and the woman staggered back, stunned by the strike upon her own chin. The

Cobra was on his feet in a moment. He reached out to seize the woman, grabbed the fabric of her mask and yanked it off. He stopped in mid-strike, jaw dropping open, at what he saw.

The most beautiful face he had ever seen was glaring at him with utter hatred. She snarled and a hand darted toward her belt. The Cobra saw the hilt of a knife and came back to reality. As she attempted to stab him, he slapped the knife away. He grabbed the would-be assassin by the arms and tugged her forth, pulling her hard up to his chest. Pinned by his grasp, the girl struggled valiantly.

His right eye burst into fierce, electrical life. "Tell me your name," he ordered.

"No!"

The Cobra bored deep into her eyes, willing her to speak. "Tell—me—your—name!"

* * * * * *

Natalya Blackova looked into that glowing marble and could not tear her eyes away. It—it was the most beautiful thing she had ever seen. She felt it slipping into her mind. As it did, all her thoughts seemed to melt away, all her hate and fury. All she had to do was tell him her name. Tell this...great man her name. Obey his commands. Obey all his commands. *No...no....* She fought it, fought the urge to worship him. So she—spat into the Cobra's right eye.

He snarled, threw her across the grove, and wiped his eye as Natalya hit the ground and moved toward her, clearly intending to kill her there and then. Natalya rolled over and turned, facing her enemy. She knew then she had little hope of survival. But she would not go down without a fight. And she would die with a smile on her face.

* * * * * *

She smiled at him.

The Cobra took a step back, stunned.

You shall know them when they remind you of your childhood, the old man had said.

The smile. The *smile*. His smile. Sanderson's smile. Her smile. Slowly, the Cobra lowered his arms. He placed his boot upon her stomach, pinning her down. At that moment Magnus Khan and a few others burst into the grove, having finally caught up with them.

"Master. Are you all right?"

"I am..." the Cobra began, but stopped. For the first time in a long time, he had no words. He gazed down upon the vision of beauty staring balefully up at him. What–what was he feeling right then? Suddenly it was difficult for him to think. He felt–he felt bewildered. Uncertain what to do next. He had never met anyone like her before. "Who are you?" he demanded.

This time the girl chose to answer. "I am Natalya Alexandria Isabella Blackova. And you murdered my parents. I will kill you for that."

The Cobra grunted. He could not remember killing any Russian couple. But wait–now that he examined her, he could see something in the lines of her face, something in the shape of her nose.

"Ah," the Cobra said. "The man I knew as Mikhail Dragovich. You are his daughter?"

"Yes. And I will kill you."

The Cobra looked deep into the girl's violet eyes. "No," he said at last, lifting his boot off her. "No, I do not believe you shall."

"I will kill her for you, Master," Magnus Khan said eagerly, reaching for the dagger at his hip.

The Cobra was silent for a long time. "No. No, she interests me, Khan. I wish to know more first. Take her away."

"To Adi Abeto?"

The Cobra shook his head. "No. My private prison. We will have words there.

* * * * * *

Natalya was sick and dizzy, lying on the rough bench of the cell that was much, much too small to comfortably serve as a bed. She had just enough strength to reach the chamber pot in the corner, where she had expunged most of her last few meals since recovering consciousness. She knew full well what they had given her, but hadn't expected to react so badly to it. Sodium Pentothal. Truth serum. Heaven alone knew what she had told them before they tossed her in here.

Painfully she blinked against the cell's sole source of illumination, a lone dim light bulb slowly losing its power. Eyes watering, she forced herself to a seated position and tried to regain mastery of herself. All right. Her attempt on the Cobra's life had failed. She had accepted that possibility when she had abandoned her home and job, risking the fierce ire of the faceless man to pursue her father's killer. Now she would be the one to die instead. So be it.

She apparently had been detained in the Cobra's own private prison. For what purpose? Torture? Rape? A painful, horrifying death? Perhaps all of the above. It no longer mattered to her. She would just have to accept it. Natalya did not believe in Heaven or Hell. She knew she would never see Papa and Mama again in any world beyond. But at least she and they would be at peace. And she had tried to avenge them.

"Ah. You are awake."

So lost in her own thoughts, Natalya had not even registered she was not alone until the Cobra spoke.

"Greetings, Blackova," the titan said calmly. "I trust you are finding your surroundings comfortable? Well–I know they are not, but there is little to be done about that." He smiled as he spoke.

Natalya glared at him. "Why did you not kill me?"

The Cobra leaned against the wall, arms folded. "Because of something an old man in Haiti told me once."

"You talk in riddles."

"That is because I am still not yet certain just what he meant. But I believe I am beginning to."

Natalya snorted and sat back down. The Cobra drew closer to the bars of her cell. "You told us much under the influence of the serum. We know everything about you. But tell me...why did you wish to avenge your father?"

Natalya was actually shocked at the question. "You have to ask me that? I loved him."

"Hmm..." the Cobra said. "What was it about your father you loved so much?"

"Why–" The Russian beauty could not understand why he was asking her such fool questions. "His love. His compassion. His strength."

"Strength?" the Cobra asked. "What is strength?"

Natalya was nonplussed. "What do you mean? Strength is just that. Strength is strength."

"Really?"

"Yes. No. I mean–love is strength. Compassion is strength. Strength is the ability to care. My father had strength."

"Did he?"

"Of course he did!" She was getting angry now.

"I would say not. You say love is strength. Did your father show you love?"

"Yes. All the time."

"Time? When was he there for you? How often?"

"He was away often, but he also...also..."

"Yes?"

"Damn you," she spat. Yes, her father had been away *far* too often.

"I thought as much. You say he was loving, that he was compassionate. Yet you know what he did for a living. How many people did he show compassion to while killing them? Where was his love for his victims?"

"He did it for the People!" she cried out, and instantly regretted doing so. It was a faceless man line if ever she heard one.

"Ah, yes. The People. The stupid, sheep-like people who never heard of your father, never knew who he was, and could have cared less if they did. Did the People ever thank your father for his service? Did they ever cheer that it was he who ensured they slept safely at night in a worker's paradise? I think not. And you, Natalya Blackova? Did the People ever thank *you*? You told us of your work with the K.G.B. The K.G.B. serves the People? Really? Or is it actually a small cadre they serve, doing what they do for their own enrichment? What was this faceless man doing all this time?"

Natalya was silent. The Cobra's words had hit a nerve.

"You hate this faceless man you work for, do you not?" the Cobra continued. "You hate his anonymous face, the fact he never tells you his name. You hate him, not just for what he did to your father–your family–but for what he did to you.

Yet he has something you have not. Power. Is that not so? You hate him, you would like to kill him, yet you cannot. And I will tell you why. Because you are too weak."

"No."

"Yes. That is what power is, Natalya. The ability to take what you want when you want. The ability to dominate weaker beings both body and soul. That is what I have. That is even what your faceless man has, of a sort. That is what your father did not possess."

Natalya clenched the bars in her hands and glared at her captor.

The Cobra sighed. "Tell me...Natalya. What do you think your father's last words were?"

"I know my father. He called out my name. My mother's name."

"Poor, deluded creature. He did no such thing. I know, I was there. His final words were: 'For the People!' Not you, or your mother."

"You lie," Natalya spat with venom.

"I do not. Your father loved sheep more than he loved you, my dear. That is a fact. Think on that." The Cobra shrugged and brushed himself off. "Get some rest," he advised. "We shall speak again."

Natalya could only look at him curiously. "Are you going to kill me? Enslave me, take over my mind?"

"No," the Cobra replied after a short pause as he turned to go.

"Wh–why not?"

The Cobra cocked his head over his shoulder. "Because I do not believe there is a need to."

~ Chapter 13 ~

"We spoke much in the days that followed, Khan, Natalya and I. She was clearly surprised at my refusal to kill her. But I had seen her smile. The same smile I gave as a boy. The same smile Sanderson showed me. The old man had been right...had always been right. I did find the only two equals to me in all the world, and both did change my life. Forever."

"Forever, Master," Khan babbled, continuing to repeat random words uttered by the Cobra.

"She would not speak back to me for many weeks," the Cobra went on. "But, eventually, she began asking me questions. About life. About power. About why the world cast the compassionate aside and rewarded the ruthless. I told her. I told her it was because power was all that mattered. All men knew it. Most simply did not wish to admit it. That was because they did not have power, and their enemies did. I knew she was listening. After a while, I released her from her cell, confined her to a room elsewhere in the palace. We continued to talk. She told me of her past. I told her of mine. Later, I extended her freedom to an entire hallway, gave her some simple tasks to do. She did them. And we spoke more."

"Tasks, Master. Tasks."

"The day she slapped a servant for dropping a dish, I knew I was getting through to her. The day she asked to join my organization, I was delighted. The day she first called me Master, I exulted. Natalya Blackova rose quickly in my ranks. She could hardly do otherwise. As the years progressed, she became my greatest asset–yes, greater than you, Khan. You were still of import to me, but my Natalya–she was my crowning jewel. In more ways than one. She stole for me. She killed for me. She planted bombs, unleashed nerve gas, slaughtered hundreds–all for me. Because she had come to believe in my vision. Because she knew I was the one destined to crush this sorry world beneath my boot and wished to be there to see it."

"Master...I know...I know..."

"Yes, Khan. I realize the rest of my story is known to you. But I yearn to tell it all, after all these years. I need to tell it in its entirety." He paused a moment before continuing. "After a time, I found the location of my new headquarters. Ironically, back in my old home village in Iran. The villagers there had not seen me in years–yet they still recognized their true master. The long-held fatwa against me had never been rescinded, but all had ceased to try and claim it long ago. The authorities knew better than to provoke me. All was well. We went back–you and I and Natalya–to the cave where it all started. There we placed the statue of Pashmir. He would serve as a pseudo-sentry to my nerve center. We blew and hollowed out the rest of the mountain and spent months in construction and the placing of equipment. I worked alongside my men, laboring just as hard as they. This would be my sanctum, and I would have my own blood mixed with the mortar."

"Blood...blood..."

"At last we finished. With the computers and communications equipment, I could contact my slaves anywhere in the world in an instant. With my library and information center, I could research whatever I needed in my quest for control. With my logistics and tactical area, I could make my plans and set into motion my schemes. In my Throne Room, I could sit and govern my empire. Yet...I was not content. Part of it, I admit, was the continuing existence of my mortal enemy. I had believed he was dead. But I later became aware of some sort of masked vigilante haunting an American city, fighting crime and corruption like the cloaked and cowled do-gooders of old. Usually I dismissed tales of such things, regarding them as no more than urban legends. But when I heard of the power this one possessed, I knew– knew– it was Sanderson, alive and well. Wielding a power that should have been mine."

"Power...power..." Khan rambled.

"According to rumor," the Cobra went one, "this masked man, this...Wraith as he apparently called himself, bore upon his body strange icons of mysterious power. Power that judged the criminals he fought, either incapacitated them or changed them into gibbering morons, in such condition as you now find yourself, Khan. Regretfully, I could do nothing about it then. I had too many other matters to attend to. So I reluctantly placed our ultimate contest on hold. But I knew there would one day be a reckoning."

"Reckoning...reckoning..."

"Yes, Khan. But while I toiled, building my empire, other matters soon took hold of me. I had promised to never let another into my heart. But soon, my heart was filled, despite my vow, in a way I never felt possible. Natalya had said it herself: 'Love is Strength.' I disdained her idea then. But the more I pondered, the more I realized the truth: yes, there was power there. Yes, it was the ultimate thing in the world. But perhaps–just perhaps–there was more, too."

"Love...love..."

"That very night I went out and stood before Pashmir's statue. I knelt and told my brother all. His emerald eyes glinted in the moonlight. Then I felt a warm wind gently blow by me, and I knew my brother had released me from my vow. I rose and thanked him. I swore to him that the words upon the memorial were true. Then I turned around and went to Russia."

* * * * * *

IRAN - FIVE YEARS EARLIER

Natalya Blackova came into the great Throne Room and bowed. "Master. You have returned sooner than I anticipated."

"So I have." To Natalya's great surprise, the Cobra was not sitting upon the golden throne from which he summoned most of his subjects. He was standing at the door as if waiting for her.

"How may I serve you?"

"There is nothing I need at present," the Cobra replied solemnly. His cape was drawn tight against his torso, covering his left arm. Natalya pondered the reason for her presence there. Her master appeared...almost nervous.

"I have a gift for you," he explained after some moments, throwing back his cape. In his hand he held up a simple white cardboard box, tied with twine. "A reward for your many services to me." He handed it to her. "Open it," he said. "Please."

The Master had never said please to her before, nor to anyone else to her knowledge. Natalya was more puzzled than ever. The box felt heavy. Curiously, she shook it gently, and something rattled within. She untied and opened the box. Even someone as experienced in horror as her could not help but gasp at what she saw.

There, wrapped in tissue paper, a face stared lifelessly up at her. It was a head, a human head. The faceless man's head.

"I hope you like it," the Cobra stated simply, as if he was gifting a spouse an anniversary present.

"I-I-" Natalya stared down at the head with a mixture of horror and glee. Moments later, the horror gave way to sheer joy. "Master-why?"

The Cobra appeared almost shy at that question, which surprised Natalya even more. "Because I wished it," was all he said.

"But...but..."

"And because..." he paused. "...I love you."

Natalya could not believe her ears. Through the many months of their talks-heavens those talks-a feeling had grown inside her that she had often wondered was love. She had never been in love, knew not the sensation the rest of the world spoke of and experienced, and knew such feelings were anathema to her master. But now, his demeanor, his words...she did not know what to think or say.

Before she could think, the Cobra smothered her with a kiss, deep and passionate. She reciprocated, standing on tiptoe, and wrapping her arms around his muscular frame. They sank to the floor.

"There is something else that remains," the Cobra said at last when their lovemaking was through. Both lay naked, exhausted, covered in sweat. But the Cobra forced himself to his feet and pulled Natalya up beside him.

"What is that, Master?" she asked.

He looked seriously at her. "To be by my side, fully, you must be my equal. As much as you possibly can be, that is. A portion of my power will be yours."

"But, Master, how?"

"In truth, I cannot explain how I know this, but...somehow, the knowledge is there. Take my hands."

She took them.

"Now gaze into my eyes. Do not be afraid."

Natalya did so. The white of the Cobra's right eye began to shimmer and glow. Soft, pulsing, and enchanting.

"I do not take over your mind, Natalya. But look deep. What I have, what power pulses through my soul, I now share with you."

Suddenly, the Cobra's eye blazed with blinding illumination, searing itself into Natalya's brain. Her entire body convulsed as an electric shock plunged into her from head to toe. The Cobra grasped her hands tightly. She felt something course from her lover's body, through his eye and through his hands, traveling into her body, her nervous system, her very being. Another convulsion and she threw her head back with a scream. She fell back, but the Cobra caught her. For a moment she was afraid she would lose consciousness. As quickly as the shock and pain began, however, it was over. The light in the Cobra's eye faded. Gently, he helped her to her feet. And Natalya knew she had a power all her own.

"My lord," she whispered incredulously. "I am like you now?"

"You have a portion of my power, yes," the Cobra said. "Its exact nature and strength will become known to us in due course. I will train you in its use. You will hone your new skills. Master them."

Natalya dropped to her knees, paying homage to her lord. "Master...I thank you."

The Cobra smiled. "I have all the reward I need in you, my Natalya. And now, my Empress–give your first command."

"Command, my lord?" Natalya replied, rising and sliding against her lover's muscular torso. "My first command to you, my beloved Master–is to come to me. Love me. Love me."

They spent the next day and a half in bed, their passion neverending.

* * * * * *

"And at last I was...whole, Khan. My Natalya filled the void within me. The loneliness I would not admit, even to myself, after Pashmir perished, was assuaged. With the ancient power flowing through mine and Natalya's bodies, with my genius and her ruthlessness, my illicit kingdom thrived. Through force, connivance or hypnosis, I gained more slaves and agents than I ever had before. My fingers reached into all the corridors of power in the world, legal and illegal. I own the hearts, minds and souls of Congressmen and Parliamentarians, dictators and presidents. Hollywood actors bow to me and spread my message in their movies and on television. Some of the most celebrated, and most despised, personages are my loyal servants. Many do not even know it. They serve as sleeper agents, living their own lives until I summon them to my side."

"Agent...agent..." Khan mumbled.

"My successes in the slow takeover of this planet were many. I have overthrown the governments in a dozen countries. I have caused terror and fear in dozens more. September 11, 2001 was one of my greatest triumphs. That fool Bin Laden had no idea he was under my influence. I wonder, when the sniper's bullet finally found him, did he snap out of his control long enough to realize what I had done to him? It would have been amusing to know."

"Master, please," Khan begged, though what he was asking of his master, the Cobra knew not.

"My slow but assured ascension to worldwide domination, I felt sure, would soon be at hand. But I knew one man would stand in my path. A wraith was haunting me, as the old man had said. Sanderson–The Wraith–would have to be dealt with."

* * * * * *

IRAN - FIVE YEARS EARLIER

After more than a day of intense, non-stop passion, the Cobra and Natalya lay in their huge bed, entangled in each other's arms. She had fallen asleep. The Cobra himself stifled a yawn as he gazed up at the ceiling. He was well pleased. Content even. In his life, all things were finally coming together. It would still take some time, he knew, but in his very soul he felt he was finally on the cusp of the fated destiny he had seen in his vision so many years ago. It would just take a little more time, such a small amount of time...

"Master."

To knock on the door of the Cobra's private quarters during the day was rare. To pound upon it in the middle of the night was unheard of. Natalya snorted and opened her eyes. "Wha–?" The concentrated pounding continued.

"Master!" the voice of Magnus Khan called out in alarm once more. "Master, wake up. You have been contacted."

"Contacted? You dare barge into my chambers over so trivial a matter? I shall..."

"But, Master... they used our own bandwidth," Khan pleaded. "From a place called Metro City."

Now, the Cobra brightened. That city meant volumes to him. It was the home of Paul Sanderson. The Wraith. "Did this person leave a name? A reason for contacting me?"

"A Robert Latham wishes to meet with you," Khan explained. "To discuss a pest control problem in Metro City."

~ Chapter 14 ~

"And that is what lead me to this city. And to my greatest defeat."

"Defeat...defeat..."

"Robert Latham. I had never met the man, but I knew the name. Head of the largest crime cartel on the American East Coast. Fingers in anything and everything illegal. Drug smuggling, gun running, international slavery. Like so many other criminals I had known over the years. And, like so many others, he was a little man. Pathetic. Fancied himself above the law, in control of others. Pah. His power paled in comparison to mine."

"Power...power..." Khan whispered.

"Robert Latham was nothing. Is nothing. A gnat. But I felt intrigued by his summons. I agreed to assist him in the elimination of our mutual enemy. But I exacted a price from him, whether he agreed to it or not. Latham would do anything to rid himself of The Wraith, I felt. Metro City would be mine for the taking."

"Metro...Metro..."

"But I did not do it for Latham. I did it for myself. I wanted to hurt Sanderson, to destroy him, body and soul. And I did hurt him, Khan–I know I did. For to injure The Wraith you cannot simply physically harm him. The status of his personal body is of no consequence to him. To hurt The Wraith, to really make him suffer–you must harm those he protects. I succeeded in that most admirably. But it wasn't quite enough."

* * * * * *

METRO CITY - FIVE YEARS EARLIER

"Master. We have failed."

The voice was a despairing wail, a cry bereft of the slightest hope. In response, the Cobra lashed out with a vicious backhand, sending the terrified Magnus Khan flying across the airship's bridge. Khan pounded against the hull and tumbled to the corrugated floor. He stared upward toward the Cobra and Natalya, pain and despair in his eyes. Beads of blood dribbled off the corner of the Mongolian's lip. But he said nothing more.

Natalya smiled contemptuously. The Cobra was enraged.

"I do not fail–ever," he roared even above the noise of the airship's engines. "We are simply falling back and will again strike forward terribly when the time is right. True, The Wraith somehow managed to ascertain a way to break my sway over those cretins sooner than I had anticipated, but that changes nothing. It only delays the inevitable." Snarling, the Cobra whipped his back upon his servants to stare darkly out the cockpit window. Then he saw his handiwork, and his spirit lifted.

Far below, the city screamed as flames roiled through the streets. For a moment, the Cobra pretended he could hear the piercing wail of a hundred sirens, the ear-splitting cacophony of a thousand alarms. The staccato rap of a million gunshots and the uncountable cries of an infinity of terrified children. It pleased him. Like the storm swiftly approaching from the east, splitting the night sky with electric-blue flashes, he had brought thunder and fire to Metro City, and his ancient enemy had been helpless to prevent it. The Wraith had bloodied him once again, it was true. But he could not halt him, never halt him. Destiny would not allow it. Yes, they would regroup at their valley stronghold established before he had met with Latham, and would return quickly to wreak further havoc upon Metro City. Upon The Wraith. He swore it.

Nearby, Natalya deftly manipulated the airship's controls, licking her lips in anticipation for the greater chaos undoubtedly to come. She was a true equal to a living god, the Cobra thought. He gazed at her admiringly.

Klunk.

The echo reverberated through the cockpit like a chill shudder. Natalya shot a quick, panicked look toward her master. Khan's eyes widened with horror. All knew what that sound indicated–that something had just struck the outside of the dirigible. The Cobra nodded knowingly. "He is here."

Just then, The Wraith burst into the cockpit. Khan, no doubt anxious to prove himself worthy in his master's eyes, was the first to confront him. "Time for round two," The Wraith said, and the fight began. Khan lashed out, but The Wraith, clearly exhausted as he was, easily avoided the even weaker man's blows. One punch, and the Dread Avenger of the Underworld finished the battle. Khan lay once again upon the cockpit floor, unconscious. The Cobra could only watch, knowing full well it was Fate that they should battle together one last time.

Natalya could do nothing to help, for the craft had just experienced some slight turbulence. Her full attention was needed at the controls. As the Cobra wished it.

"It is fitting to finish this here, above your beloved city," the Cobra told his nemesis. "We are the only two worthy to hold her in his hands. It is indeed fitting to fight for her here in the stratosphere."

His enemy snarled. "You let others fight your battles, you flee like the coward you are. You are nothing. Metro City will never be yours."

And at those words, despite himself, the Cobra felt himself flinch. Those words reminded him of his childhood, from the bullies that used to menace him so. Their words now echoed in his brain.

Goosaleh. Goosaleh, stupid little goosaleye goh...

"Then let us finish this now," the Cobra growled. The Cobra, like his namesake, sprang for the kill. Strangely, The Wraith's speed failed him. Perhaps he was simply too exhausted from his previous endeavors to avoid the charging figure. Either way, the hero was unable to prevent the Cobra from barreling into him, sending both careening into the far wall. The Cobra reached out, entwining his fingers like iron ropes about The Wraith's throat. He slammed the Dread Avenger back into the wall again and again and felt a thrill as he realized his ancient enemy was losing consciousness. Enthralled with the joy of the potential kill, the Cobra yanked The Wraith back one more time and thrust him once more toward the wall with all his strength.

Too much strength. The wall of the dirigible was thin, made only to keep the surrounding environment out. The constant pounding against it of two heavy bodies, both at the pinnacle of human strength, was too much for it. The metal tore and gave way. Then both spilled out into empty sky and the approaching storm. The winds whipped about them as The Wraith gripped the dangling rope ladder. Gritting his teeth, the Cobra clung to the foot of his hated adversary as their bodies swayed uncontrollably, directed freely by wind and the erratic movements of the dirigible above.

Closing his eyes, the Cobra willed the power surging within him to strengthen his own grip. But that was not how his abilities worked. His grip loosened. He had to hold on, he simply had to. His destiny was not yet fulfilled. He was the Cobra. Destined Master of the Earth. All that knew him was fated to bow to him. His fingers tiring, memories flooded his mind, coming back to him in a cacophony of images and sound.

Pashmir's fanged, bloody face appeared before him. Beautiful, faithful Pashmir. His first and greatest friend. His brother. He saw the Ayatollah, that fool. Then he was back in Africa, watching as the serpent-worshippers slew his only friend. He saw himself back in Eritrea, and on the mountain, fighting *him*. Sending the fool to the ground like the weakling he then was. Then the old man of Haiti's words rung out loud and clear.

Either you shall ascend into the heavens—or you shall not. And if you do not, the only way to go is down.

Down.

The Cobra peered upward, and saw his enemy looking down at him, even as the masked vigilante struggled to hold on himself. He nodded to himself. It was time to let Fate decide.

"Did I not say," he cried out to his foe over the storm, "it was fitting to end this here? Indeed, though it is not the end I anticipated."

As his words were drowned out by the stark winds, his grip on The Wraith's ankle faltered...

...and he fell.

He never screamed on the way down.

~ Chapter 15 ~

His story almost over, there was silence in the cell for a long time. The Cobra sat in quiet reflection, the memories of a lifetime washing over him. At his feet, the drooling, piteous remains of Magnus Khan wriggled worm-like, spinelessly begging for his master's affection. The Cobra ignored him for a full five minutes. Then he spoke. "It was fortuitous that we were flying over the harbor. Striking the water at such speed was like colliding with a steel wall. Any ordinary man would have perished instantly. But I am no ordinary man. I managed to contort my body, and punched through the water much as a high-diver does into a swimming pool. Yes, I was wounded...but I would heal in time. I had men stationed throughout the harborside. They retrieved me, and we retreated to another of my nearby strongholds. I was in no condition to do anything."

"Condition...condition..."

SERPENT RISING | 149

"I spent months recuperating, unable to even speak or move. But I learned of my beloved Natalya launching her attack of vengeance against The Wraith. You were there as she did so, there when he destroyed her. Destroyed the only being, save Pashmir, I ever loved. And you, Magnus Khan, let him expose you to his power. You let him turn you into the pathetic imbecile that cringes even now before me, while Natalya lies in the grave he should be in!"

"Master...forgive me..."

"Forgive you. Forgive you!" His voice grew to a roar. "The Wraith shall yet fall at my hands. He shall live just long enough to see everything he stands for, everything he loves, ripped from him as he ripped all from me. Even now, my plans are in motion to destroy both him and his city. Vengeance, the ultimate vengeance, will soon be mine." Carefully the Cobra rose, smoothed out his cape, and readjusted his tunic. Then he took a deep breath and was about to continue.

"Master...master..." Khan begged again.

"Of all those who have served me across the years, only three have been truly loyal to me–Natalya, Pashmir, and yourself. Rest assured The Wraith shall pay for what he did to my Natalya. And to you." The Cobra took a deep sigh. "I shall indeed miss you, my friend." He reached out and gently, placed his hands on either side of Khan's neck. With a quick jerk, the Cobra snapped Magnus Khan's neck. The body hit the floor with the sound of a sack of wet cement.

After some moments of silence, the Cobra stepped over the body, and walked out into the corridor. "You. The one called Jess." Slowly, with a robotic step, the slovenly guard shuffled forward. His red, triple-jowled face was blank and emotionless. The Cobra regarded the corpulent zombie with undisguised contempt, directing him to follow into Khan's cell. "You have a pistol?"

Jess nodded. "Yes, Master." He brandished it for his lord to see.

"Then demonstrate its use upon yourself."

The obese guard obeyed. The blast was deafening in the crowded confines of the cell. What was left of the security guard soon joined the remains of Magnus Khan upon the cell floor. Next he turned his attention to the nurse Lydia Hughes. Dispassionately he regarded her entranced beauty. He ran his eyes up and down her slender form, then nodded. "You shall accompany me. Although many turned away while I was wounded, there were yet those who remained faithful to me. One did me great service during my convalescence. You shall be among his rewards."

"Yes, Master," the girl droned obediently. Mechanically, she fell in behind her lord as he strode majestically out of the cell back into the hall.

They were not interfered with on the way out of the hospital. The Cobra had taken care of that. The next morning the day shift would find two bloody bodies in Khan's cell, a missing night nurse, and several staff members standing around with blank expressions and no memory of the previous night's events. There would be accusations of drug use in a state-funded hospital and calls for an investigation. Then the Director would simply grease a few official palms, fire a few supervisors, perhaps frame one or two of them, and all would be well once again.

This was Metro City. It never changed.

The Cobra emerged into the cold night and traversed the steps to the sleek black limousine waiting for him. A chauffeur moved to open the door, but the Cobra motioned that he should put the entranced Lydia in the front first. He had no further desire for company that night. "Home," was all he said.

The limo door closed, leaving the Cobra in darkness. A moment later and he heard the engine purr smoothly into life. Then they were moving, out of the gates of the asylum and through the near-empty city streets.

Silently, the Cobra gazed out of the tinted window at the great spires and towers of Metro City. In the east he could see the purple blob of the emerging sun slowly redden as it rose. As the color fleshed out, it seemed to him like a great arc of blood looming over the metropolis, threatening to burst and drown its buildings and people in a crimson flood. The thought pleased him very much.

I know you are out there, old enemy, he thought. *I know you are waiting for me. You shall not have to wait long. But when we do next meet, it is I who shall emerge the final victor. And then you shall truly know the strike of the Cobra.*

~ Author's Note ~

I hope you enjoyed this never-before-told origin tale of The Wraith's arch-nemesis, the Cobra. Both this book and its companion story, SANDERSON OF METRO, have long been in-the-works. I wrote both some years back as comic book stories, intended as a 2-part graphic novel. Part 1 was released last year, and was illustrated by Jake Bilbao. Part 2 is scheduled for release either this year or next.

As I was writing other Wraith books at the time both SANDERSON and SERPENT were being worked on, I enlisted two pals of mine, and superb writers in their own right, Bobby Nash and Greg Gick, to help me flesh the comic scripts out into full prose format. I think they did an excellent job. Both did a full first draft, and then I completed the job when time allowed.

As such, I'd like to thank Greg here first and foremost. Through the hardships of life, he laid out a truly compelling, heart-wrenching story based on my original comic script. His talent and hard work helped make this book what it is today. I cannot thank him enough for that. I'd also like to thank my wife, Jennifer, and our soon-to-be-born daughter, Emma (she'll be arriving in two days time, as I write this), they are my everything; and our family and friends, for always being there for us. And special thanks goes to Malcolm McClinton, who painted the wonderful cover to this novel, and has become my new go-to artist for future painted covers. Thanks buddy.

The next book in The Wraith Adventures series will be KINGDOM, and it picks up right where the previous novel, VENDETTA, left off. You can see a special, unedited sneak peek of chapter 1 of this upcoming novel, in the following pages.

I hope to see you next time, and God bless my friends.

Frank Dirscherl
Wollongong NSW, 2019

KINGDOM

~ Sneak peek ~

Turn the page for a preview of the next novel in the series, *Kingdom*, by Frank Dirscherl.

COMING SOON from Glowing Eyes Media

~ Prologue ~

"Honey, hurry up. It's coming on now."

Leena Patterson's voice carried through loud and clear from the living room into the Sanderson House kitchen, where Paul Sanderson was trying to make a quick cup of coffee for the two of them.

"Don't worry," Paul said, a mug in each hand as he entered the cavernous and plushly decorated living room. "I doubt it's anything too important. Latham Industries is probably just announcing a new CEO to replace Patrich Azufi. Or perhaps they're going under."

"Surely not," Leena replied to the last portion of his statement.

Paul sat next to her on the leather couch, handed her a mug and gazed at her while she stared wide-eyed at the large screen television on the opposing wall, waiting for the press conference to begin properly. Her long, strawberry-blonde hair was tied back in a ponytail, and her blue eyes sparkled in the light. To Paul, his fiancée looked like an angel.

"There, it's starting at last," Leena said eagerly.

Paul took a sip of his Breakfast Blend coffee and ruminated on the recent past. Over the past few months, Metro City had been largely devastated by the villain Crossfire, whose mad schemes of revenge saw the loss of countless lives, most notably those of crime lord Robert Latham, his erstwhile lackey Charlie Grieco, and Latham's short lived successor, Patrich Azufi. And now, on this fine Sunday afternoon, a formal announcement on the future of the company was commencing on live TV. Paul would have rathered been out and about on such a gorgeous, sunny day.

"Mayor Hutchison is about to speak," Leena said with a hint of surprise. "What does he have to do with Latham Industries?"

Paul looked on but remained silent. *Now* he was interested in what was about to be announced.

"Ladies and gentlemen," Hutchison said into the camera in a stern voice, shifting his short, rubicund body somewhat uncomfortably, "as you know, this city has seen its fair share of tragedy in recent months. Gang violence, terrorist attacks. Many innocent lives lost, including my good friend and this city's patron, Robert Latham. Since his death, and that of his protegé, Patrich Azufi, the company has naturally suffered. Its stock price has plummeted, offices have shuttered, jobs have been lost. And, this city's fortunes have waned along with that of this fine company."

"He's laying it on thick," Paul said, rolling his eyes. "Even if the company is folding, it's hardly worthy of such a grandiose public declaration."

"However," Hutchison continued, his face brightening slightly, "amid all the doom and gloom, I can hereby announce there is hope. Hope for Metro City. Latham Industries is on the precipice of a new age of success and prosperity. Its destiny is to carry this great city forward along with it, as it always has in the past."

"Oh please," Paul blurted, rolling his eyes once again.

"Only one person can guarantee such an outcome. Now..." Hutchison continued with his narrative, pausing briefly for effect, smiling the entire time, "...this will no doubt come as a great shock to you all. It did to me only yesterday. But it has also brought me great joy...which I know you will all share with me. I am so very pleased to announce the CEO of Latham Industries, the man who is ready, willing and able to rescue the company, and the city as a whole–"

Paul sat bolt upright, his eyes bulging.

"–is actually its original CEO; its founder, and this city's great patron, Mr Robert Latham!"

Paul couldn't believe what he was seeing or hearing. He felt numb, as though he was suffering from shock, and he felt sure his jaw had almost crashed against the floor. He looked over to Leena beside him, who appeared as stunned as he was. There, on the television in front of them, hobbling into camera, was indeed Robert Latham, his great nemesis. The man looked appeared older, somehow, and he needed a cane to walk, but the expression on his face–in his eyes–confirmed his identity at once.

The Wraith's enemy lived!

About the Type

Garamond is a group of many old-style serif typefaces, originally those designed by Parisian craftsman Claude Garamond and other 16th century French engravers, and now many modern revivals. Though his name was written as 'Garamont' in his lifetime, the typefaces are generally spelled 'Garamond'. **Garamond Normal**, used in this book, is one of those modern revivals.

~ Also Available ~

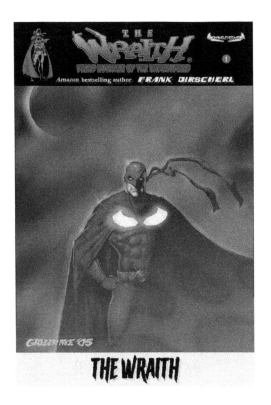

The Wraith Dread Avenger of the Underworld #1
THE WRAITH
Frank Dirscherl

In a world not far removed from our own, a city lies ravaged. Crime overruns its streets, its citizens are helpless. Crime lord Robert Latham holds the city in his sway. One man, however, stands above the rest, willing to fight for freedom. That man is The Wraith!

NOW AVAILABLE!

www.glowingeyesmedia.com

The Wraith Dread Avenger of the Underworld #2
VALLEY OF EVIL
Frank Dirscherl

After the horror the Cobra unleashed upon Metro City, Paul Sanderson has recuperated, regained his strength and focus, and the city has been rebuilt while its citizens have slowly started to regroup and move forward. Into this relative calm marches Ma Tzi, the Hong Kong drug lord, who senses a weakness in resident crime lord Robert Latham's hold on the city and intends to exploit that in any way necessary. And at any cost.

NOW AVAILABLE!

www.glowingeyesmedia.com

The Wraith Dread Avenger of the Underworld #3
CROSSFIRE
Stephen J. Semones & Frank Dirscherl

After a terrorist attack leaves the citizens of Metro City reeling, an enigmatic stranger emerges from the wake of the destruction to wage war on local crime-lord Robert Latham. In the midst of this, Max Horton, The Wraith's right-hand man, vanishes without a trace. Searching for Max, and for those responsible for the devastation, The Wraith sets out for answers.

NOW AVAILABLE!

www.glowingeyesmedia.com

The Wraith Dread Avenger of the Underworld #4
CULT OF THE DAMNED
Frank Dirscherl

With the city back firmly in his grasp, crime lord and entrepreneur Robert Latham is celebrating by bankrolling Metro City's 200th anniversary gala year, which includes the unveiling of a never-before-seen ancient Aztec stone carving—the Cortes Stone—at the City Gallery, a carving that has thrilled the scientific and artistic communities, but infuriated the monstrous Aztekoth.

NOW AVAILABLE!

www.glowingeyesmedia.com

The Wraith Dread Avenger of the Underworld #5
CRY OF THE WEREWOLF
Frank Dirscherl

Having gone through ordeal after ordeal, Paul Sanderson (aka The Wraith Dread Avenger of the Underworld ®) and his love Leena Patterson, decide to take a long overdue vacation. However, their idyll is soon shattered by an attack by a creature nobody thought could possibly exist—a werewolf. Soon, an evil so heinous makes himself known, and only The Wraith could possibly defeat it.

NOW AVAILABLE!
www.glowingeyesmedia.com

The Wraith Dread Avenger of the Underworld #6
SWAMP WITCH OF SATAN'S FOREST
Frank Dirscherl & Ray MacKay

On their way home from their mountain vacation which was anything but, Paul Sanderson (aka The Wraith) and his love Leena Patterson are waylaid by a mysterious cry for help, and are unwittingly drawn into the forest—and the web—of the alluring Swamp Witch.

COMING SOON!
www.glowingeyesmedia.com

The Wraith Dread Avenger of the Underworld #7
VENDETTA
Frank Dirscherl

After having been betrayed by crime lord, Robert Latham, and defeated by The Wraith, Crossfire has returned to cause mayhem and carnage at every turn. His ultimate aim? The utter destruction of all his enemies, and he doesn't care who gets in his way.

NOW AVAILABLE!
www.glowingeyesmedia.com

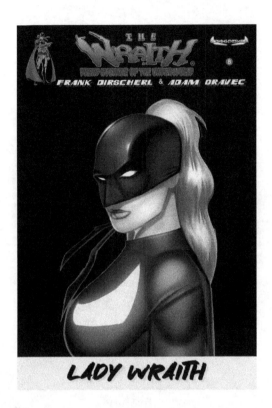

The Wraith Dread Avenger of the Underworld #8
LADY WRAITH
Frank Dirscherl & Adam Oravec

The Wraith is missing. No one has seen him since going out on patrol. Now, the love of his life Leena Patterson, must sally forth on her own as Lady Wraith, protect the city, find her love, and combat a deadly new adversary hell-bent on destruction.

COMING SOON!
www.glowingeyesmedia.com

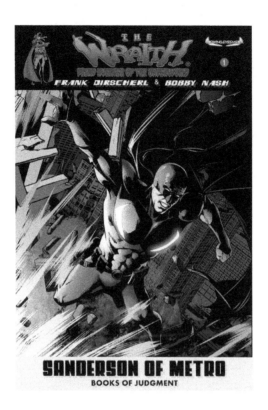

Books of Judgment Book One
SANDERSON OF METRO
Frank Dirscherl & Bobby Nash

Two masters of the pulp fiction world, Frank Dirscherl and Bobby Nash, have come together to tell this tale, the secret NEVER before told origin of the first Wraith/Paul Sanderson, as only they could. This action-packed, atmospheric thrill could only be told now, and it could only be told by master storytellers like Dirscherl and Nash. An epic never to be repeated and not to be missed.

NOW AVAILABLE!
www.glowingeyesmedia.com